She is an impossibilit   _ thought. So tall, and utterly intriguing, from the spiral signet hammered into her breastplate, to the large, jangling sack she carried effortlessly on her back. Her burnished red hair that hung around her shoulders and the length of her back caught the sunlight in a blaze of fire. So serious, but Kirstine's dreams had been filled with the rare smiles that changed her eyes from ice to warm summer sky.

Impossible, yet here she was, walking across Kirstine's hall with the ghostings of that intriguing smile on her otherwise stern face.

Praise for Karin Kallmaker

Velvet in Venice, Coin of Love Book 1

A tiny touch of magic makes everything better, even an already perfect romance... [Karin's] love for food, travel, music, and sapphic women is clear with every word in this book. Add to that a touch of magic in the form of a mysterious coin and you have the perfect romance. Favourite badge! – *The Lesbian Review*

Highly recommended for a drama-free, sweet, and adult love story set in a gorgeous location. My rating: five stars!" – *MG Digby, Goodreads*

Cowboys and Kisses

This story is so much more than a historical romance because it portrays the harsh realities of life for women on the frontier who didn't have any money or family to protect them and it also shows that passionate interludes can set someone's heart on fire but love is the only thing that will keep the blaze going. ...A touching and steamy historical romance... – *The Lesbian Review*

A love story that sticks to your bones. – *Reader at Kindle*

I fell in love with Darlin'. Her tenacity, her staying power, her not letting go of her hopes and dreams. It's a gritty book, but there is a fine balance between romance and reality. And the intimate scenes are beautifully appropriate for the period. I highly recommend it. f/f Kallmaker blew me away. 5 Stars! – *Lez Review Books*

I was so drawn in by the story that I tore through it on a Friday and then spent weekend rereading it, slowly this time, so that I could take my time and savor the story as it truly deserved. That reading this gave me great pleasure will not surprise anyone who is familiar with Ms. Kallmaker's work, however, what I did not anticipate was that I would be so moved by how she illuminated the realities that most women endured in this time period. It was impossible to not feel my heart ache for plight of the main characters and yet so, so satisfying and cathartic to see that they were allowed to have their happy ending. – J-Dog at Kindle

Simply the Best

One of the things I love in Karin Kallmaker's books is the way she sets the scene. Her characters have real jobs, not just titles mentioned here and there. It's part of who they are, part of the story, almost akin to world-building in sci-fi or fantasy. – Rainbow Literary Society

Get this book if you want to believe that anyone can find love, even if they don't necessarily believe in fairytales. Get this book if you love good writing, excellent chemistry and something a little different from the main characters. – The Lesbian Review

Because I Said So – Goldie Winner!

These characters have depth. There is also a great deal of chemistry, especially between Kesa and Shannon. Their attraction crackles with electricity from their first meeting to the last page. She is obviously skilled in writing great stories, and this book is a great example of her work. – Rainbow Reflections

...A well-written plot with innovative character drama and a love story that doesn't disappoint. The romance sparkles, the characters are enchanting, and their struggles are fascinating. – Lambda Literary Review

Touchwood 30th Anniversary Edition
What a beautiful book. I now understand why *Touchwood* is a favourite for many readers. I stepped so deeply into this story I feel like I have spent the afternoon in Louisa and Rayann's bookstore. – *Eh at Kindle*

Touchwood explores... with a deft, sensitive touch. It's a wonderful book...truly outstanding. – *Bay Windows*

My Lady Lipstick – Goldie Winner!
Karin Kallmaker...delivers a perfectly plotted and paced contemporary romance. She's a true master of the craft, and this book is not to be missed. – *Curve Magazine*

...A well-written plot with innovative character drama and a love story that doesn't disappoint. The romance sparkles, the characters are enchanting, and their struggles are fascinating. – *Lambda Literary Review*

Painted Moon 25th Anniversary Edition
Abby Craden's fine narration brings it all together. The extra two short stories in this anniversary edition tie a lovely bow on the ending. Mandatory Lesfic reading! – *J-Dog at Kindle Whispersync*

The extra chapters at the end were FANTASTIC! – *Andrea, Reader Review*

Knight

of

Nights

Karin
KALLMAKER

Romance and
CHOCOLATE INK

Cover design: Karin Kallmaker

Editor: Heather Flournoy

Published by Romance and Chocolate Ink

This story is dedicated to Emma Thompson, Lizzo, and Michelle Yeoh: three women who point out artificial limitations on their lives as women and artists and say, "No."

Thank you Katherine Forrest, for your gentle guidance to the baby writer I once was. Without your example my career would have gone in different — and unsatisfying — directions.

Thank you for an honest review or rating of this story. You make the book world turn.

Aphaea Artemis lays her hand on the world.

Groves of olive, pastures of sheep, clusters of humans guided by her wisdom, She who hates ignorance and want. She who rewards strength tempered by care.

She created me for the Beloved, immortalizing her own and the Beloved's faces. Her heavy arm hammered the tendrils of her power into every line and facet of me. I was made for the Beloved to mark the beginning of Forever. I am the promise between two equal spirits.

After I fell into the Icarian Sea and was carried on the backs of Poseidon's seahorses to distant sands, I knew not my purpose. My magic had no one worthy to receive it.

Carried over sea and land, I sense her hand in verdant pastures and hear her voice in bells and harp strings. In a dark land a green sanctuary exists. Where green grows, rot follows. When light shines, darkness hungers for its extinction.

I have no power over the turning of the world, so I follow the pulse of the Goddess, traveling toward those whose devotion to light and life deserves reward.

Chapter One

There had been rustling in the wood for the past three days. She knew the difference between foxes on the hunt and two-legged clumsiness.

"They're back."

"You've healed well, my girl." Breda set a large clay bowl in front of her before joining her at the long sturdy table, most of which was covered by a winter weaving project nearly done. "But I still believe your head took more beating than you think."

She warmed her hands in the steam from her supper stew. "That's as may be, but I am not wrong about this. There is someone out there. From the smell, not the same someone as last evening. I should roust them out."

The mass of tight, kinked gray that surrounded Breda's head like a halo bobbed as she considered the suggestion. "It could be someone too shy to ask for my help."

Only at night and for several nights in a row? She thought not. She kept her counsel because there was no point in repeating last night's argument about it. She pulled the heavy blanket close and dug into the dowitcher and turnip pottage. The serving was as generous as the round curves of Breda's figure, and every bite warmed her. She'd hoped to catch a rabbit for their supper, but a bird had sufficed — Breda was as good a cook as she was a healer.

Though she remembered nothing of her life before waking up on wise Breda's cot, she knew that food this hot and rich was uncommon. She was grateful for the older woman's kindness and hoped her help with everyday chores and overdue repairs had evened the scales for the hospitality she consumed.

Breda was right; her head did still ache from time to time. She didn't remember the blow, but the clear dent across the side of her helm matched the bruise she could still feel from temple to ear. How had her foe not finished her off? How far had she walked in a senseless daze? A long way, it seemed, given the state of her boots. A *very* long way, even, because Breda knew of no clan that kept women in their soldier ranks.

Of her appearance she knew only what her own eyes could see, or Breda could tell her — she was as tall as most men, and mayhap closer to forty years than thirty. Her face, Breda said, looked as if she'd been born scowling at the world. Her eyes were gray or light blue, depending on the light, and fringed in thick black. The pinpoints of freckles against skin, as pale as Breda's was dark, covered the front of her body. Breda said they were just as plentiful on her backside. The single braids twisted from each temple were of long-ago weaving and lacked any shine of health. The bangs forever getting in her eyes appeared to have been cut with a spoon, at least in Breda's judgment.

Time, Breda preached. Busy hands freed the mind. Her history would come back in time. Yet, three weeks and a day later, not even her name had returned to her.

A twinge at her temple reminded her of the futility of forcing memory. Her name might elude her, but she'd learned a great deal about herself, hadn't she?

She knew how to clean and repair her armor. The iron scales and chain link were far from new, but the bronze seal on the breastplate, helm, and shield said some expense had been undertaken in its making. The spiral seal was known to Breda as a symbol of life, older than time itself, but Breda knew of no clan that used it. The same was true of the engraved runes and letters on her axe blades and handle — Breda had no idea the people they were made by, though their general form and shape was like that of Norse tribes and clans.

When she stood quietly in a clear space and held her axe at ready, her body remembered a swirling dance of steps and lunges that made her axe sing in the air. She knew how to throw the thin dagger sheathed in her belt with enough skill to pin a falling leaf to the tree behind it.

She hadn't flinched from the gore when a local man had staggered in streaming blood from his thigh after falling on his plow. She'd handed Breda a thin strip of leather to tie above the wound before Breda had even asked for it.

She walked as if she'd spent much of her life astride a horse, and she knew both bridle and saddle knots, which came in handy trying to keep the troublesome goats tethered at night. She did not know the knots that Breda used for the same tasks, knots that Breda said were used by sailors. She was certain that she had never milked a goat nor a sheep, but hunting small game and foraging for firewood she did easily and well.

She had no name. But she knew she was a soldier, not a sailor, nor a farmer. She was also practical and useful, and she would eat anything put in front of her. The rest will come, she told herself.

After supper she joined Breda for a survey round of the small huts and lean-tos that ringed the grove sheltering Breda's small holding. They lured the chickens into their roost and set the doors and hatches against night visitors. The repairs she'd done to the hut held nicely, forcing the foxes to find other meals. While Breda applied a fresh poultice to a cut on one of the goat's legs, she made sure the tethers holding all three goats were well secure. As usual, one of the three head-butted her onto her backside, but she nearly forgave them because Breda laughed so heartily.

She stood some way off while Breda checked the door of the drying hut, which was filled to its rafters with early spring chervil. It was Evil's own weed, she had decided, because she sneezed whenever she was near it.

On the other side of the grove, near the two sweet chestnut trees, she smelled an intruder again. She grimaced in the direction of the source, but all was still.

"I don't like it," she said as they both worked in front of the fire, her rubbing paste polish into the thin iron scales on her boot covers. She knew they should be bright as scales on a silver fish, but at some point, rust had set in. "They are closer every night. Why would someone watch you? Or are they watching me?"

Breda's dark, wrinkled face was as steady as a standing stone that faces sun and wind and gives back warmth and safety. Her gnarled hands never paused in their threading of her smaller loom. "You have no reason to think they wish either of us harm."

"They're attempting to be quiet. They're bad at it, that's the truth of it. They don't know the wood and therefore are either reckless or stupid. Neither is comforting to me."

"It will be as the goddess wills it."

She grunted. Breda's goddess was not one she thought she knew, and Breda's acceptance of Fate without challenge didn't sit well on her mind either. She was grateful and comfortable in this place, but it did not feel like home.

As the fire waned, they wrapped large, heated stones in thick wool and tucked them into their beds. Breda's pallet was on a four-post platform no wider nor longer than she was. Her own bed was on a low cot where folks who'd come for healing could rest. The pallet was stuffed with tufted wool and goose down. Its softness was a comfort, as were the hot stones at her feet and another at the small of her back, between her and the cold wall.

Her body liked these simple pleasures, but every night as she fell asleep, she was aware that her hips weren't used to such ease. Covered by two blankets, she drowsily worried that she'd sleep too well, and the presence she sensed in the woods might find advantage in that.

She was of an instant full awake. Not sure what had startled her, she rolled to her feet and reached for axe and shield. Leaves rustled by a night-feeding marmot would not wake her.

The sound came again — the scuff of a boot on packed ground.

Without thought, wearing only the shapeless night shift of Breda's that strained at her shoulders and reached only to her knees, she flung open the cottage door and stepped into the moonlight. The low moon cast faint shadows that made trees into thin giants.

As she set her shield on her left arm, she shifted it to reflect what there was of the light. *Let them see who I am.* Her right hand wrapped around the carved ash handle at its midpoint, she swung the axe in an arc around her head so the twin, curving blades would catch the moonlight too. In one continuous, smooth motion, she brought up her shield so the edge of one blade slid across it, sounding an eerie note of iron menace that silenced the wood around her.

Words, deeply known, came to her. "I am Skyra of Stane. Declare yourself!"

Leaves rustled, much farther away, and again farther. She listened until the wood was full only of night noise.

"I am Skyra of Stane," she repeated. She had a name.

PART ONE

Lady Kirstine
of Castle and Clan Drummoch,
born to the Meic Lochlainn,
descended of the Fairhair Ui Neill

Chapter Two

"Can you yet see their sail?" Kirstine kept her own gaze fixed where she'd last been able to tell the white flutters apart from the gray horizon.

Behind her, Lachlann exhaled so heavily his breath stirred the fabric of her hood. No doubt he was out of patience because she had asked him this five times already. "I think I can discern it. They have not turned around."

She finally asked him the question that had lived in her from the moment she'd realized her husband was considering this utterly mad plan. "What odds do you give them?"

"The same as all adventurers."

"Androw is his own lord, but I wish Cannmor hadn't gone with him."

"Where Androw goes, your eldest follows."

"It makes no sense to me. None of it." She still could not believe that Androw had taken up the call from the Norse king to ride to the other end of the world, and for a god he only held up to regard when an hour's piety could be followed by feasting and revelry. But he had. At least only one of her sons was with him.

She shaded her eyes from the midmorning light. She could see no sail returning either. With Androw gone beyond even Lachlann's long sight, she might relax, a little.

"It's a crusade to glory," Androw had said when he pronounced the venture at court and called on his chief landholders and their sons to support it, join him, or both.

A fool's crusade, as far as she was concerned, and her husband was often a fool. She nearly said so to Lachie but thought better of it.

Androw, Lord Drummoch, the great fool. He and a half dozen lords with another dozen sons had left the clan with spring nearly upon them, and for what? A distant so-called Holy Land. She held little hope of seeing any of them again. If they did return, it could be two years or more. Meanwhile, she would rule the clan in Androw's name, train their second son Galdring when he returned from fosterage next year, and do her best to protect them all from winter hardship and summer raiders.

Her sigh might have been why Lachlann hastened to add, "Your lad Cannmor was fostered well. He's strong and used to life on horse or water."

"Androw is no longer used to it."

Now Lachlann took his time to answer, as was her half brother's way when it might not be politic to agree too quickly. He knew Kirstine's feelings about her marriage, but Androw was yet Lachlann's own lord and benefactor. "Your husband is reliving his youth — the days when he won you, Sister."

"You mean before he accepted sheep, iron, and peace, along with me, from our father. No doubt he'll win the hearts of other maidens." Dryly, she added, "He can still raise his sword, unless there's wheat-ale."

Lachie smothered a laugh. "These Drummochs, they know how to make ale."

"True, what you say." That was why she herself poured him a cup of the rare, potent brew most nights. She would not survive another pregnancy — the last had nearly killed her. The Green Woman had said so. Her next natal day would be numbered thirty-six. With Androw gone, the last thing she needed was a confinement and suckling babe. Androw's empty tower rooms were doubtless eyed by the ambitious.

Shading her eyes, Kirstine shifted her focus to the bailey below her, no longer able to ignore the call of her duties. Though the rains had finally eased several days ago, there was still mud everywhere, including along the bottoms of the rough stone walls that enclosed the main keep, barracks, forge, and stables.

The half-empty stables were being mucked out, and the smell was likely powerful. Dried grasses were churned into the deep grooves and many hoofprints left by her husband's departure. The wagons that had been heavy with grain, ale, and weapons to provision the Norse-bound ship were trundling into the lower bailey, their round trip to the port completed.

It was left to her to replace the provisions Androw had taken for this glorious crusade. Chief among her worries was that there had been only a faint stirring of spring at

Imbolc and lambing had begun early during heavy rains. Beltane would be soon upon them, and the eastern fields were only last week sown with seed.

She calmed her worries by recalling her joy yesterday at the sight of tight bumps of green on the branches of the lone crab apple tree in the keep's garden — a hint of spring, at last, but so late.

The winter had been lean, and the storehouses for the castle and the townsfolk beyond the wall in Drummbhaile were near bare of grain and fodder. That there was anything left at all was a matter of pride to her. The autumn she'd arrived as Androw's bride had been followed by a dire winter of starvation and sickness that all seemed to accept as Fortune's levy upon Clan Drummoch.

She had not accepted it. Storehouses were filled when there was will to see it done — it was obvious, just as water was wet. Hunger was an enemy that could be fought, but Androw in his heart was no farmer. In that first year of marriage, however, he'd been greatly enamored of her, and she'd secured his support to see to it herself.

Harvest storage and winter rationing were foreign ideas, however. Twenty years ago, it had taken the threat of Androw's sword to enforce her plan. Now most of the clan, even those in remote hamlets, had seen the value of fore-planning in the bodies of their children grown tall and strong.

Mayhap Androw's fit of madness, taking him to the other edge of the world, was her reward for the lives she'd saved and mouths she'd fed. Mayhap, if she believed any gods took an interest in her. As a sold-off, third daughter of faraway Galrandel, she had no reason to think any god cared.

For whatever cause of Fortune, Androw was gone from her sight. Today, that was all that mattered.

Tonight she would lock the door of her bedchamber. The idea was so delicious that she shivered, making the stiff wool of her outer dress rustle.

"We can go in if you're chilled."

"Not yet. The sun is wonderful."

Lachie's boots moved restlessly on the gray and white stones patterned at their feet. "Court is waiting."

"I know. A moment more." It was a rare indulgence. There were those of her husband's Drummoch people who still saw her as a Galrandel foreigner. She'd learned their language and song, and all the sacred and customary ways of the folk, from farm to green to kirk. These twenty years of ceaseless labor, including that of producing three living children, had earned her grudging tolerance from the more pragmatic and practical clansmen, and mayhap a measure of respect. She was counting on their support during her time as steward.

She took one last, deep breath of the sweet, warming air. The tang of a mild sea was on it. Like everyone else, she eagerly awaited the return of the first nets with the long-lived and generous sturgeon that would fill bellies and replenish larders with stock and mealfish. In turn, full bellies meant plowed fields, repaired grazing walls, shorn sheep, and turned millstones.

It also meant the energy for family life and celebration. These Drummochs knew how to celebrate, this all the gods knew. The fishing boats were due back a week today and Beltane was shortly after. The midwives would be busy nine months hence.

The Lady's Watch, set facing the castle gates and the road down to the town, was above most of the aroma of the keep and bailey. It was her favorite place in her husband's world. Even Androw and Lachie asked before joining her on the narrow balcony adjacent to her rooms. Legend said the first chatelaine of Castle Drummoch had used it to watch for the return of her lord. It was a romantic notion, but Kirstine doubted she was the first lady to use it to make sure her lord wasn't coming back — at least not today.

She knew Lachie well enough to feel him deciding whether he should clear his throat to remind her of the passing time. She turned to him before he did so. "Laze-about, what are you waiting for?"

He made a disrespectful noise with his lips. "After you, Lady Kirstine of Castle and Clan Drummoch, born of the Meic Lochlainn, descended of the Ui Neill, and a right sheep's arse."

She laughed at him as he treated her with a grandiose bow, still feeling blessed all these years that he'd accompanied her to her wedding and somehow never found a reason to leave. Even after his wife and children were lost in a disastrous shipwreck, he had stayed. His humor and sword, both dark and bloody, had strengthened her all these years. Those who'd teased him about his shortened right arm or his then landless state learned why his sword was called *Dread-Mordad*.

Halfway down the narrow spiral stairs, cut out of the rock that formed the keep's seaward defense, she noted that the stone smith had still not mortared an ice-made crack. He'd put her off a month ago saying the stone was yet too damp to hold a repair. The weather was finally in their favor, however. She'd insist. If there was one lesson she had tried to teach Androw and any Drummoch who would listen, it was to pay attention to cracks. The cracks in stone, fields, fences, mill wheels, and especially in people.

At the base of the stairs, Lachie put his shoulder to the heavy door that secured the sleeping chambers and Lady's Watch from the rest of the keep. They startled a boy trying to catch a chicken, and Kirstine was relieved to pick up the welcome scent of seed bread wafting up from the kitchen.

Behind her, Lachie abruptly shouted, "Oi! You there – piss on your own wall! We have privies, ya ass." He clouted the shoulder of one of the clanguards flanking the door to the tower. "I shouldn't have to tell you to haul him down to it!"

She wrapped her plaid closer around her shoulders and left him to his cursing. Lachie was as fastidious day-to-day as he was deadly when angered, and the general cleanliness of Castle Drummoch was hundredfold better than when they'd arrived. A person could walk without slipping in the muck of dogs, cats, and chickens. Dried, sweet rushes strewn on the floor were as valued by her as grain boiling in a pot. She no longer went everywhere with her nose buried in sprigs of sweet chervil she'd found in the then ill-tended castle garden.

As she pushed open the door to the great hall, the raucous shouting she'd heard from outside fell silent. Her skin puckered in gooseflesh as she considered the many eyes following her path to the raised dais and her husband's chair. Her thin white hood was properly pinned to her hair, and she fought the urge to check it. Though her dress and smock were the same simplicity as always, she'd fixed her warm plaid to her shoulder with the heavy clan brooch Androw had left in her care.

Her hand on the oaken chair's heavily carved back, she surveyed the room. The petitioners weren't too many for weekly court. At the end of the hall was a short line of folk bringing in belated tax portions. Clever, sharp-eyed Una was busily writing in the accounts ledger while her father, Benneit the Seal Keeper, sent eggs, barley, peat, and the like to the various larders.

The court petitioners' faces were a mix of emotions. Some showed plain their mistrust in her justice or their cocksure belief that they would prevail. Others held close their feelings with as much skill as she did, content to wait and see. She would choose one of those first.

Lachlann said she was all silk and pillow feathers that hid a heart of iron. Today, some would see her iron heart for the first time and not be pleased. She had no sword of her own and only her wits for a shield. For women, she knew, it was ever thus.

Chapter Three

Before Kirstine could sit in the lord's broad oaken chair, Benneit waved from his cluttered clark's table and pointed at a thin, dark-edged young woman. His nod meant he believed it would be quick and pleasing to Kirstine. He'd signaled the same to Androw to begin court days, and she was gratified the Seal Keeper had chosen to do the same for her. Why would he not? After fifteen years as Androw's clark, his ledgers told him every day that the clan prospered.

Expecting to bless a new birth or agree to a handfasting that had taken place weeks ago, she made her way to where the young woman was huddled on a stool.

She sprang up as Kirstine approached, quickly ducking her head in respect. She'd obviously scrubbed her face and hands, but her hair and mud-spattered cloak hadn't been so fortunate. "Lady, I thank you for a moment of your time."

Kirstine extended her hand to invite the touch of the girl's fingertips to hers. "Why have you come to court?"

"Not to court, Lady. To see yourself. I am sent by my mother." She ducked her head again as she drew a small purse from under her smock that was hung around her neck with a long, much knotted string. "By my mother who passed two months ago. She wished me to bring you this."

The purse was flax made and no broader than a birch leaf. As she reached for it, Kirstine reminded herself that Benneit had heard the story behind the offering and trusted it. "Thank you. Have you had a far journey?"

"Two days' walk, from Oakenbrae."

Memory stirred. "Was your mother Alyss? Alyss near the high loch?"

"She was. I am the babe she told me you saved."

So long ago. How had the years passed so quickly? The girl was at least sixteen. "I am pleased to meet you again. What are you named?"

"Alyss, like my mother."

As they spoke, Kirstine untied the heavily knotted string of reed that appeared to have remained so for many years. From the weight, she expected a rune stone. Instead, something unexpectedly uniform and flat tumbled into her hand. Metal, but tarnished with salt and age.

Looking down at the object in her hand, Kirstine asked, "And what is this?"

"She would only tell me she found it years ago in a pool where the loch becomes river, and that the moment she touched it she was reminded of you. She kept it all this time, intending to bring it, but time was not her friend."

"It's no friend to most of us, though sometimes it is kind."

At that, young Alyss smiled, and Kirstine then recalled the mother's face. It had been desperate with pain, afraid that her belly would split before she could deliver. Kirstine had managed to turn the babe and it had slipped into the world. Looking at the healthy, vocal child as Kirstine had placed it on her chest, the mother's face had lit with that same smile her daughter now wore, as if she knew a happiness no sorrow could take away.

Kirstine had envied that smile, and she envied it still. "I was as frightened as your mother, I think. I'm no midwife, and I'd only seen it done once. Was pure chance my riding party was close. The Green Woman would have been too late."

"My gran, rest her soul, didn't know it could be done." Her eyes brightening with pleasure, Alyss added, "I deliver babes and lambs good as the Green Woman now. She's taken me for student."

Pleased that the child she'd saved was doing such powerful work, Kirstine allowed herself an indulgent smile. "That's wonderful. I'm sure your mother was proud of you. Was her passing hard?"

"Ma, when the medicines no longer soothed her, asked me to ease her way. Da held her close and I brewed the herbs. She passed peaceful and finally free of cursed pain." Young Alyss pressed a hand to her breast. "I do miss her."

She was only sixteen, Kirstine reminded herself, to know so much of life and mercy. She studied the begrimed object again, then slid it back into the purse and tucked it into her own pocket. A rush of confidence filled her. A lovely keepsake and omen on this, the first day of her stewardship.

With a glance at Benneit, she asked, "Do you think anyone here is leaving tomorrow in the direction of Oakenbrae?"

Clever Una, ever at her father's side, and about the same age as Alyss, answered. "There's a farmer going home to Oakenglen. Mayhap she can travel with him that far. He was mostly clean and very polite." From Una, the last part was high praise.

Alyss perked up. "Is that Blue Thomas, I wonder? He's been gone a week."

"His name was Thomas, yes. He brought pounded flax and is taking two large stone." Una's narrow face split with a merry smile. "He was a bit blue."

Alyss rolled her eyes. "He's never got a coat. Hasn't the wits of a babe. He'll be with his ox and wagon trying to keep warm."

From the smile lingering on the girl's face, Kirstine was certain that young Alyss welcomed the journey with Thomas. How kind of Fortune to bring them a gift of time together after Alyss's faithful duty to her mother's wishes. "Stay the night here in shelter and dine you both at table tonight."

"Lady, thank you. My mother's grace and blessings on you!"

Una gestured at Alyss to follow her to one of the small cot rooms off the kitchen. The two put their heads together and giggled.

Kirstine could scarcely remember being that young.

She glanced at Benneit and found his gaze on her, along with an encouraging smile. She took a deep breath and turned to the dais again.

Chapter Four

By midafternoon, Kirstine was weary, but the easy disputes had been dealt with. A ewe in the wrong field, a dowry not paid after handfasting, damage to a cart on a track ill-maintained by the landholder — such matters were clear, often requiring only her promise to uphold the law they all knew. Give the ewe back, deliver the next born ram to the new son-in-law, fix the track and also the cart, or else.

Androw had usually been vague about the precise meaning of "or else," and she was as well.

The final petition before her was the most difficult of the day, but the hall was mostly empty now. If she stumbled through the law and diplomacy for a solution, the witnesses would be few.

She carefully listened to the statements of a freeman landlord and his bound serf. They agreed on what had occurred during the winter. The serf had at Mabon delivered his landlord all harvest that was due. Then the freeman had taken the entirety of the serf's remaining harvest after Yule, leaving the family to gleanings, winter fishing, and the pity of their equally hungry neighbors.

The law was on the landholder's side in near every regard, but all the gods knew that no clan survived without able bodies willing to work.

Kirstine put her hand to the clan brooch on her shoulder to needlessly straighten it and was glad to see the gaze of the freeman drawn to it. "So you do agree that your serf yielded the proper portion owed from his harvest?"

"Yes, he had done so. But my family hungered." The freeman scratched his russet beard. "It was mine to take."

"Of course." The freeman was gaunt, no doubt of that, as were many after the long winter. The serf was ever more so. "Tell me, though. Next winter, when your family hungers, whose harvest would you take then? Your man here doesn't look able to bring a full yield from his farm."

He shifted nervously. "I can replace him at the holdings with someone who can."

She saw the stooped and shaky serf take a shallow, nervous breath. "Sir, you realize that if you continue, you'll soon have no harvest at all. Then your family will truly hunger." Before he could answer, she asked of the serf, "How large is your family?"

"We are ten, Lady. The elders can help some. The youngest is four."

"Eight hungry mouths to feed? Get your mistress to speak with a midwife, man."

His head bobbed as he pulled at his forelock. "She has, Lady. Twill be Christ's miracle if we have more."

There was laughter from the scattered onlookers at that, most of it not unkind.

She encouraged the humor by laughing herself even as she inwardly sighed. Androw would have humiliated the freeman for greed and the serf for laziness, which would solve nothing. She didn't think either was true. However, she had observed that embarrassing those with rank in front of those without was dangerous — mayhap not for Androw, but it would be for her. This freeman had enough bluster to resent his serf winning any concession, and he would, no doubt, take it out on the serf even as he resented Kirstine.

"This is my judgment. There is no wrongdoing." The serf's eyes filled with despair as a smile of satisfaction blossomed on the freeman's face. "However, Clan Drummoch will not survive if we do not all survive together, as our Lord Androw has so said. I judge that any freeman who deprives a serf of more than the agreed-on share will redeem that excess with two day's full labor by his own hands at planting."

The freeman did bluster, but she soothed his ire by adding, more quietly, "Use those days to show your serf the quality of good, hard labor, and observe in him and his family their deep knowledge of their holding. Try you both to find ways to increase the yield of his harvest. Doing so makes your lands stronger. We need not fight ourselves for food if we work together."

He frowned mightily but nodded.

She called to Benneit. "Did I see a basket of barley brought in?"

"Yes, Lady. Una has it here."

"Give it to this man." She raised her voice. "And let no one seek to take it from him." To the serf she offered her hand, and he pressed his forehead to it in a babble of thanks. "Your work and your family matter to Clan Drummoch. Regain your strength and serve your lord."

The serf hurried to collect the food, leaving her alone with the freeman. She extended her hand to him, and he quickly pressed his forehead to it. That was a good sign. She leaned closer to him and said, lowly, "Do not send someone in your stead. I promise you, break ground with your people to make a bond deeper than the law. Teach this to your children. And I praise you for keeping a midwife close."

He gave her a glimmer of a smile at that. "My lady sees to all. I care not what the kirk says, too many mouths to feed is weakness, not strength. I will do as you have said. To honor your generosity to him, I will send a clutch of eggs within the week."

"Brightly done, and I thank you for your care," Kirstine said, and she sent him on his way.

By the time the scullery maids and footmen came in to arrange and set the tables for supper, she was tired and yet pleased. While taking tea and resting in her rooms she allowed herself cautious optimism. Court was a test of tenacity. She'd managed her first day without obvious blunder. The highborn court with nobles the day before

Beltane would no doubt be full of intrigue and grudges, but she had nearly three weeks to gird herself for it.

She returned to the great hall in a plain but fresh linen kirtle and red cloak to find the tables ready. Some of the guests, servants, and castle laborers were already seated in hopes of an early pouring of ale. They were at *her* tables, she reminded herself. She spied young Alyss and her Thomas at the table nearest the door. He was indeed a bit blue.

Androw's chair had been pulled to the rear of the dais and set atop four small stools so it could be seen from every corner of the room. It was swathed with the bright red-and-gold clan tartan and embossed with the clan thistle in thread of gold. The Rock of Drummoch, marked with the blood of Raghnall the Great, anchored the cloth as it proclaimed Androw's right of rule. She would use Androw's chair for court to underscore his authority, but she'd decided to keep her own chair the rest of the time.

The wives and children of several of the men who'd left with Androw were seated to her left and right. Supper was mutton broth stew, simple but hot and plentiful, and fortified with thick chunks of trooping fungle that distracted from the sparsity of meat. Glad to feel warmth in her hands, Kirstine focused on her food and, as was her habit, let the chatter of the ladies eddy around her ears without much comment from her.

They talked mostly of babes and marriages, and their hopes for the coming crops and an end to strict moderation when the sturgeon came in. After lingering with seeming interest for a second pour of ale, she feigned growing weariness. At least she hoped she seemed tired, even as a pronounced tingle behind her stomach grew each time she contemplated her first night truly alone for so many, many years.

Stopped thrice on her way to the tower's door — horse master, kitchen steward, and Captain of the Night's Watch — she finally made her way through it. The tower's ground floor was occupied by the most noble born of the guests. The second floor was for family, which included Lachie, and rooms set aside for the children. Her daughter, Gunnhild, had her own home now. Cannmor had gone with Androw. Only Galdring would have need of the rooms when his final year of fosterage ended. His latest letters, though, suggested that his heart might be happiest where he was.

Lachie's rooms were lit, and his valet murmured, "Good sleep, Lady" as she passed. He bowed his head at her usual response of, "And to you."

Three-quarters of the top floor of the tower was Androw's bedchamber and council rooms. The rest of it was hers. Up the final flight of spiral stairs she went, letting her cares about cracks and hungry bellies drop away with every step.

Marial, her maid, quickly stowed the broom she was using to sweep dust from under her cot in the antechamber. "The fire and lamps are lit, and the warmers are wrapped in fresh wool. Your robe ought to be warm now too."

"Be off to your supper, then." Marial was easily Kirstine's favorite maid over the years. She was a quiet girl with a sturdy and sensible way about her. Of a sudden she had to blink back tears of gratitude. Marial's competence had pushed out the overstated need for other attendants. It had taken years of subtle control, but she'd finally rid herself of the petty circle of ladies-in-waiting who only waited on jealousy and useless gossip. A circle that had never yielded anyone who wished to befriend the foreign wife from Galrandel. "A couple of lads were singing with a fiddler when I left, and they knew their tune better than most."

Marial quickly lifted Kirstine's heavy cloak from her shoulders and bustled to the inner chamber to hang it up. She returned in moments. "I will enjoy that, thank you, Lady."

"If there's fresh water, I'll not need you until the morning."

"There is, Lady, and the usual half ale. The fire kettle should be hot, and the tea steeping cloth is on the table if you should wish some. Of course I will be back by the Night Watch bell." Marial, who attended the kirk, always expressed shock at any suggestion she wouldn't return to her own bed, alone, at evening's end. "It's yet too cold to sing all night."

"I'm not sure the lads will notice the cold."

"That's because they're always thinking about ale. Most of them, anyways. Your chambers are as you asked, I hope." With a duck of her head, Marial took her leave, and Kirstine listened to her boots thumping quickly down the stairs.

Kirstine closed the antechamber door but left it unlocked for Marial's return. Her own door, tall and narrow, stood open. The silver light of oil lamps and the orange glimmer of the fire beckoned her inward. She left the door open as she toured her sitting room and bedchamber and peeked out on the Lady's Watch. There was no one in all that space but her.

She returned to her door, set her shoulder to it, and pushed it closed. The latch fell into place with a hard, square thump. Over it she fastened the stiff iron hasp and pushed the final spindle through.

For a moment she fancied that her spirit lifted from her body like a glissando rising from a harp. The feeling left her warm and strangely hopeful, as if she would wake on the morrow to find the gardens in bloom.

Chapter Five

Standing near the fire, Kirstine unfastened the ring belt that pulled the kirtle tight at her waist. The pins holding her white coif she dropped into the bowl where Marial would retrieve them for use again tomorrow. Sitting in the wide oaken chair on wool-stuffed pillows that soaked up the fire's heat, she pulled her boot dagger free from its pocket and set it on the table, then set about unknotting the ties that bound the boots over her hose.

Marial's help would have made undressing easier, but Kirstine was more than capable of caring for her own body. She longed to do simple things for herself. To poke at the fire and dance if she wanted to. To read or simply enjoy the solitude of her own thoughts, unobserved. To wear her hair loose and uncovered, as women had in Galrandel.

She let her mind skip over loch and sea to faraway Galrandel. It would be green now, and the glens filled with the clack and grunts of plow and planting. On Beltane, the braes would resound with the clamor of flocks herded between the two fires to higher ground for the summer. The days would be rich in sunlight and the nights heavy with music. Galrandel... So much that she loved and had not seen in twenty years.

Mayhap home was no longer as she remembered. The only news she heard was from traders and Androw's heralds. The fact of her mother's passing five years ago had taken months to reach her.

All at once that sad day's memories poured through her mind. The news had been told to her by a returning herald, but he'd been given no letter or keepsake to bring to Kirstine. Why did it feel of a sudden as if she'd not cried enough then? She'd drenched her kerchief wiping away tears, and lain for hours on her bed, inconsolable. The long-ago grief felt so deep that she fancied she could hear the three ladies of lost Avalon singing a lament with her.

Why, when there was finally a prospect of hours every night to herself, did she feel compelled to visit again the past? She turned to look through the door of her bedchamber, at the marital bed Androw had visited last night, drunkenly insisting that she could still ripen with another son. Her last confinement had ended early, and death, for a time, had sat with her too.

Androw was gone, at least for now. She could give up the bitter herbs she secretly steeped into her morning tea that kept her womb empty.

She pulled up the bodice of her dress to mop at sudden tears. As a bride, she'd imagined having some leisure for her music. Of making a friend or tending a blooming garden for pleasure — of having one moment in the day that wasn't planned around necessity and survival.

Then she'd thought mayhap that time would come after she'd banished the smell that permeated the basements and kitchens. Then mayhap after her first confinement, then after the next harvest.

How had twenty years slipped away so quickly?

Homesickness grew from whisper to shout in her heart. Twenty years of it flowed out of her, and she allowed it because there would be no knock at her door, and no one to comment on her red eyes.

She knew Galrandel could not have been a green land soaked with dance and music, but her memory wanted her to think it so. It was easy to remember the past as if it were painted gold. When her own daughter had been married to sow ties with Clan Badenoch and their precious road to eastern and highland markets, she'd had naught to say about it. Androw wished it and it was done. There was a grandbabe two years in this world and yet never enough soldiers or leisure for Kirstine to see the child for herself.

Galrandel or Drummoch, it did not matter — she and her Gunnhild had been dealt the same Fate, traded like sheep.

This maundering was useless, she told herself firmly. She'd drown in her own pity if she didn't stop.

Her tears slowing, and feeling finally warmed by the fire, she rose to let her dress fall to the floor so she could step free of it. After shaking it out and folding it carefully, she carried it to the dresser top where Marial would tend to it in the morning.

The wool dress she'd worn earlier in the day had been brushed and folded, ready for tomorrow. On top was the flax purse young Alyss had brought — Kirstine had forgotten all about it. She shivered as she picked it up. It was not a night to be running about in naught but her chemise and hose.

She returned to her chair near the fire, purse in hand, and pulled on the warmed lambswool-lined robe and slippers that Androw had gifted her some years ago. Wrapped tight and shivers easing, she opened the purse and slid the metal object onto her palm. Held up to the fire's light, it didn't seem nearly as tarnished as it had earlier. She could tell now that it was definitely a coin, but whether gold or bronze she couldn't yet discern. It had been a long while since it had been bright, to be sure.

Its weight on her fingers was both heavy and cool, but it warmed to her touch quickly. A talisman, then, for this new, strange, and welcome time in her life. On impulse, she rose to place the coin on the mantel so that it leaned against the marriage cup engraved with her and Androw's signets entwined.

She had scarcely turned back to the chair when she heard the coin clatter on the floor.

"Bothersome thing." She tried twice more, but no matter how she arranged it, it rolled onto the floor. When she propped it against the vase of dried broom and sage, it finally stayed in place. Its edges where the grime was thinnest reflected a dull gleam of the lamplight.

Mayhap there was beauty under the tarnish. At first, she thought to have Marial set about cleaning it, but no.

She'd do that herself. She'd need paste polish and a brush. Time for that another day.

On a whim, she stretched her arms over her head, going on tiptoe to twirl in place. She was of the tall Fairhair, and her height equaled Androw's. He was not here to remind her that he disliked that. Her heart beat faster, in a way that rushed blood to her fingers. Her neck tingled — was this what freedom felt like?

Eyes closed, she sought her memory for a song her mother had taught her, the one about faerie sisters and the green west. She danced as she sang the couplets she could recall, happy to feel the gentler language of her home filling her mind and her mouth. Easy and light, Galrandric centered on the tongue instead of the top of the throat. It was a language so beautiful she pitied all the lands where it wasn't spoken.

Thoroughly warmed, she returned to her chair and scooted it closer to the low table nearest the fire where the thoughtful Marial had set her harp case.

Her harp was kept wrapped in oilskin and cradled in lambswool, all set in a heavy maple box inlaid with white maple and birch. Her mother had had it made for her as her blood gift. She'd been betrothed to Androw shortly thereafter and wedded three years later as the final settling of safe passage terms between the two seafaring clans in the habit of raiding each other's ships.

This instrument was the only thing of value she'd brought with her from Galrandel — not including Lachie, of course. He'd not thank her for ranking him lower than a piece of wood, no matter how beautiful or useful. Androw liked her playing, but only when she played the songs of his clan. Many summer nights she sat on the Lady's Watch, harp at her shoulder, and played so as to be heard in the courtyard below. It was too cold to sit on the Watch tonight, but she would on Beltane if there was no rain.

Her heart ached at the sight of the taut strings and the curve of the pillar. The graceful, golden willow wood was the essence of her childhood home. Even though she had added two fingers' span to her height since it had been made, it still comfortably rested on her knees and nestled into her shoulder. She was impatient to play, but first she made sure each of the twenty-six strings was tuned.

When a sweep over the strings finally pleased her ear, she fell into her mind to find the first song she'd ever learned to play. "The Lament of Egrid" was everything her young heart had craved. A handsome soldier falls in love with a princess meant for his lord. A princess so fair and good the trees wept for joy. Together they undertake a perilous journey with dark magic and soaring starlight. Love and glory, full of risk and tragedy.

The words flowed to her lips and the music to her fingertips. At the final stanza her voice finally warmed, and she let it soar. Blood on the tiller marked where Egrid breathed his last, and primrose petals fell like snow on the face of the fallen princess. They had risked and lost everything for love.

She felt of a sudden that a chorus joined her in the final, tragic verse, twining with her melody but with words she could not quite understand.

It was a sad and lovely tale. She'd spun some of the songs she knew into Androw's language, but never this one. It would reveal too much, to others and to herself, of the hopeful, romantic girl she'd once been. As the final note sounded, she was deep in the story's pain, and she could no longer ignore her own. Her voice broke, and she hugged the harp to her as she once again sobbed.

She carried those twenty years of bottled-up tears to bed, finally, leaving the bed chamber door open to take the last heat from the fading fire. She had craved solitude but hadn't expected the devastation of having it. Whatever spurred this maudlin bout, she would be too busy tomorrow for it to linger.

As she settled into her pillow, hot stones warming her feet, she realized there was a sliver of firelight where the bed curtains met. She sat up to better close them, but her fumbles instead increased the gap. It wasn't the fire catching her eye, it was a glint from the mantel. The old coin was gleaming. Was one of the lamps still alight?

With a sigh for her just warmed feet, she padded in her hose back to the other room. The lamps were all snuffed. Now that she was closer to it, the coin looked just as it had when she'd set it against the vase.

"My feet are cold again. I thought you might be a good luck charm, but you're a bit of trouble, aren't you?"

As she picked it up, she remembered young Alyss's devotion to her mother. That was a good and true thing. Her heartache of earlier eased. "If you do naught but that for me, you're worth keeping near."

In bed again, she took one last look at the coin where she'd set it on the bedside table next to her ewer and cup. The curtains tweaked fully closed, she snuggled down to warm her feet. "The Lament of Egrid" came to her mind, and she hummed it to herself as it were a lullaby.

Chapter Six

Kirstine's gritty eyes didn't seem to draw anyone's notice the following morning. Without weekly court to attend, she made a quick survey of the storehouses and stables, then consulted with the gardener on the progress of the flat beans and summer peas. Growth was steady the length of the planting with no sign of rot or pest.

Three landholders insisted they discuss upcoming Beltane rites. Once their egos were soothed about their place in the festival, she spent a short but very happy time reading a fable to the castle children to whom clever and patient Una was teaching letters and numbers.

The clarity of her purpose was steadying after the tears of last night.

As the afternoon light waned and she thought to ask for polish paste and cloth from the scullery for the coin, clever Una approached, her face showing a rare lack of confidence. "Lady, the girl, Alyss, she has come back. I don't know what to make of what she says. It seems fanciful, but if it's true..."

She pushed the coin back into her pocket. "About what?"

"They were a few hours' walk from here with their ox and cart when they stopped with other travelers to eat. There were some local men much angered at the death of some ewes, including the mother-of-herd. It sounded to her as if they blamed the Green Woman and meant her harm."

A bell of alarm sounded inside Kirstine. "You don't believe her?"

"I only doubt her judgment of what she overheard. That she believes it I don't doubt. She ran all the way back here to tell me."

"She seemed a sensible girl, and will no doubt be a Green Woman herself," Kirstine mused. "Is she in the kitchen?"

Una at her shoulder, she found a shivering Alyss huddled on a stool near the huge kitchen hearth, her head over a bowl of steaming pottage. To Kirstine's eye, Alyss seemed to have given every last ounce of herself to return with her warning.

Kirstine bade her keep her seat. "How many were there?"

"There were three, Lady, but a f-fourth overheard them and said he'd join them. Mayhap they'll find more." She pressed the warm bowl of stew to her thin chest. "They'll burn her out, and probably worse. Two were kirk folk and would blame a woman in the wood over their own g-gods because sheep heavy in winter wool don't float."

Una patted Alyss's shoulder. "It was a terrible time for all of us. Seems like everyone lost a few. Do they think the Green Woman caused the rain?"

Alyss's voice grew scornful in spite of her shivers. "They'll believe she's powerful enough to make it rain but weak enough for them to attack."

"If they wish to make war, they should do it with each other." Una's practicality asserted itself. "Take off your shoes and put your feet on the hearth stone. You should stay the night here."

"No, I want to get back to Thomas. He said he'd wait for me."

"Stay your worrying on that for now," Kirstine said. "Una, find Egann or Lachlann, whichever of them, and—"

"I'm here, Sister."

Kirstine turned to find Lachie lounging in the doorway with the look of a man who hoped to find an early taste of supper.

"I know it's late in the day, but I fear this cannot wait." She glanced at Alyss. "Which Green Woman did they speak of?"

"Breda, of the grove and loch. I've never met her, but my teacher has."

Lachie's sharp gasp matched Kirstine's as he left the doorway with a quick step. "What's this about?"

"You remember her, Lachie?"

"You don't forget a woman you tied to you on your horse."

"She saved my life. As did your wild ride to bring her. There's a group of villagers, mayhap five, some armed, and they blame her for—"

"Anything their ale suggests." Lachie's hand fell to the hilt of his sword as he turned on his heel. "Egann and I will see to it."

Kirstine hurried after him. "I'm going with you."

"Kirsty, you are capable of many things, but one thing you're not."

"Which is?" Quick as she was, she could hardly keep up with him as he took the stairs up from the kitchen two at a time.

"Changing into riding kit before we ride out."

"I can so," she protested. Curse his long legs. She picked up her skirts and ran as he loped across the bailey toward the stables.

"Egann," he called ahead. "It's time for a spot of fun."

Egann MacDrummoch had captained Androw's guard and patrol for a decade. Like Lachie, he was quick to draw sword, but Kirstine had always admired his care for his men and horses.

"You, me, and two more." In the spare language of soldiers, Lachie explained the matter to Egann, who gave a sharp command. Footman sprang into action, some fetching bridles and saddles. Others opened stall doors to lead out fresh horses.

"Saddle my mare," Kirstine said. "I'm going with you."

Egann's prodigious beard, raven black and threaded with white, was so thick only his dark, hawkish nose emerged. He said so little that if she hadn't seen him eat, she'd have easily believed he didn't have a mouth. The twitch of his eyebrows at her words voiced his opinion.

Lachie's dark eyes looked heavenward as if pleading for deliverance from foolishness. "If you're ready by the time we leave."

"You'll wait for me, Lachie!" Kirstine stopped herself from stamping her foot. "Just as you would Androw. She saved my life," she added with a hiss.

"Time wastes while you blather on."

She glared at him and made a show of addressing Egann. "Have you one more reliable man who could take a girl pillion some miles up the loch as soon as she's fit to travel? Tonight?"

Egann's eyebrows twitched again.

"There's someone waiting for her. She ran all this way to warn us. I'd spare her the walk back, and she deserves the safety of escort." Androw wouldn't have bothered to explain himself, but she did not stand on his solid ground.

"It will be done." Egann held out his arms as his squire arrived with his armor. In the sunlight it glimmered like the scales of a bronze dragon. He wasn't bothering with more than thick leathers for his legs.

Lachie was thumping his favorite gray's flanks as the footman slipped the bridle over the horse's head. "Time wastes, Sister."

She ignored him. "Is four enough?"

The question earned her a look and sigh from Egann, but he said nothing.

She quickly said, "I'm sorry. Your judgment is best."

With the scarcest nod of his head acknowledging her apology, Egann simply said, "They'll run when they see our shields."

They may run, but will they stay away? The question was in Kirstine's mind as she bolted for the keep's main door and ran as fast as she could up the spiral staircase to her rooms. Halfway up she was shouting ahead for Marial to get out her riding shift and traveling cloak. It wasn't seemly that she was half-unbuttoned by the time she crossed her own threshold, but there was no one to see but her and her maid.

It was quick work to pull on the thin linen breeches and tie them around her waist. The kirtle slit front and back was next, covered with a six-paneled riding smock that allowed her a comfortable seat without skirts bunched under her. It was more cumbersome than what she'd ever worn in Galrandel, but it was also much warmer.

Lachie had best not leave without her. The moment Marial finished buttoning the smock, Kirstine headed for the door.

"My lady, did you want these things?" Marial gestured at Kirstine's boot dagger and the coin that she'd discarded in her haste.

"Yes." Her dagger had been a wedding gift brought by Lachie from her father. She thrust it into the inner sheath of her riding boot. Short and wide, it was meant for use at table, but it had drawn blood twice — first hers and then Androw's during their wedding rites. The diagonal scar on her palm was all but gone.

She felt sorry that she'd forgotten the coin too. The pockets of her kirtle were hidden under the layers of the smock, so she thrust it into her bodice.

"Lady, be careful, please," Marial pleaded as Kirstine ran down the stairs, cloak over her arm.

"I have no intention otherwise," she called up to the girl. Breathing hard, she thought to pause and regain some composure, but Lachie was right; daylight was against them. When she reached the stable it took an effort to hide how her chest was heaving. There had been a time when such exertion would have been nothing to her — were those days behind her now?

They needn't be, a quiet voice whispered.

The truth was she had no time for daily rides and to work with Lachie on self-protection as she once had, even if Androw would allow it.

Androw was gone, she reminded herself.

It had been scant minutes since she'd left Egann and Lachie, and she was pleased to see that Lachie's squire, fostered from Clan Badenoch, was still in the process of fitting Lachie's breast and back plates to him.

Egann stood with young Timmoth and gestured to her. "Where will Timmoth here find this girl to escort?"

"She is Alyss and in the kitchen with Una. Make sure she is warm and see her safely met with her friend on the road."

Young Timmoth ducked his head and marched off in the direction of the kitchen.

"Have stew yourself before you leave. It's cold!" she called after him.

She thanked Egann and began to ask after his lady wife, who approached her confinement, but was interrupted by Lachie's laconic, "Whenever you're ready, Sister."

Her exasperated sigh drew a rare smile from Egann. "I have four brothers such as him."

"You poor, poor man." Kirstine turned toward her mare and mused that it was the longest conversation she'd ever had with Egann.

Aware that Lachie was waiting to mock her further, she set her boot in the knitted fingers of the page who stood ready to assist her in mounting.

"We can get you a high stool." Lachie mounted his gray from the opposite side. His right arm might be short a few inches, but the muscle was thick and sturdy. He'd always been as graceful as he was rude. He shifted a knee against his gray, and it obediently danced closer to Kirstine's mare.

Show-off, Kirstine thought crossly. She trusted that the page was used to lifting men stones heavier than her and, at his nod, put her weight fully on him until she could gain the near stirrup with her free foot. A moment later she was safely astride, cloak settled around her and dignity intact.

She blinked innocently at Lachie. "I've not forgotten how to ride."

"I had been thinking for some time that mayhap you had."

How long had it been since she'd been riding? All the winter ago? As Lachie had said, an evening ride and settling a matter of clear justice would definitely be a spot of fun.

You're overdue for that. Most definitely she was overdue.

She walked her mare the length of the bailey, talking to her in a quiet voice and tickling at her ears. When Lachie called to her, they trotted back and joined the party. Egann and Lachie rode out first, then her with two soldiers behind.

Egann set them a steady canter as they raced the sun.

Chapter Seven

Within a few minutes the rhythm of riding came back to her. If they faced no delays, horses such as these would get them to the glen before daylight faded. The night she had almost died, Lachie's round trip in the dark had taken an hour, or more.

She flinched from the vivid memory of that night. She'd measured time in the number of blood-soaked rags the despairing midwife flung into the rinse basin, and the hard, wracking cramps that didn't move the babe. Clan custom treated women's birthing as a mystery, and it was the one time the commanded words of a woman weren't questioned. They'd needed a Green Woman's knowledge, and quickly.

Kirstine had been barely conscious when she'd heard Lachie's strained voice at the door, so many rags and cramps later. She remembered a dark, kind face surrounded by a shock of wild black hair, and suddenly feeling wrapped in fresh herbs and rich earth.

When she'd next woken, they'd taken the too-early babe away. It was this Breda who'd quietly whispered to her so not even the midwife heard, "Never again. All the future decades of your life would be gone for a child who will never draw breath."

They took a left-turning fork in the road, and Egann quickened their pace. Her mare was at a gallop. It couldn't be far now. They narrowed to single file to make use of the best part of the road as long, deep shadows began to crowd out the light.

She'd never told Androw she shouldn't have another child. She'd told herself it was for Androw's sake she kept this secret. With the memory of that night so vivid now, she knew that was a lie. She'd feared being seen as no further use, and discovering how little he valued her work for his clan. Did he care that more young ones could read? That fewer starved? That moving privies and waste downhill from wells and streams had all but ended the wasting bile sickness that took the very young and very old?

Such measures were in the service of light and life. All the gods, anyone's god, would surely value this, else why would anyone bend the knee in worship? But not Androw and too many of his clan, quarrelsome whenever cost or convenience was challenged. Some took more care of their sheep than they did of their children. Androw — ever the soldier, never the farmer.

Arrows are not food.

There was smoke in the air. Please let it not be the holding and trees, Kirstine prayed. The wind blew back her unpinned hood. She'd no sooner pulled it into place again than long-hanging leaves brushed it once more off her head. Ahead, very close, she heard the clang of iron on iron and pleased laughter.

Lachie, in the front, urged his gray to high speed and they thundered into the grove.

"Drummoch!" Egann and the others took up Lachie's battle cry. Lachie banked left, and she followed. When he suddenly reined his gray to a stop, she veered around him and pulled her mare to a halt.

Their battle cry trailed off in confusion.

Breathing hard, Kirstine tried to make sense of the scene.

The smoke came from a fire set in one of the huts. The flames lit the clearing in front of the cottage. A burly man lay groaning on the ground, bleeding from a gash to the shoulder. Another four men — hayforks, axes, and a sword aloft — surrounded a tall figure with its back to the fire and casting a long shadow.

This armored man, near tall as Lachie, carried a bright shield with no flag or sigil Kirstine recognized, and spun a long battle-axe in one hand as it if were a feather. The knight's armor shone gold head-to-toe in the firelight, dazzling Kirstine's eyes to the point of tears.

The tallest of the attackers — the one with the sword — glanced in alarm at the arrival of mounted soldiers but nevertheless advanced with a swing of his sword in fresh attack on the knight.

Even as Egann yelled, "Hold!" the knight parried the swing with a swipe of the shield. For a moment Kirstine thought that long, double-headed axe would lop off the man's arm, but the knight instead used momentum to hook the attacker's ankle with the sharp toe of an iron-covered boot. The man thumped to the ground full on his back and bellowed an oath new to Kirstine.

Kirstine heard the laughter again. It was the golden knight who laughed.

"Hold, I said!" Egann eased his sword from its scabbard. "In the name of Lord Drummoch, drop your weapons."

The villagers complied.

The knight did not.

In a voice made hoarse by the smoke, the knight said, "I do not know this lord of yours."

"You shall."

"Lachlann, no," Kirstine began, but he was already off his horse.

While Egann's men herded the attackers into a huddle on the ground, Lachie eased his sword from its scabbard as he walked slowly toward the knight. "You'll throw down your weapon before my lady, or you'll see your arm in the mud next to it."

The knight laughed outright — oh, the wrong thing to do.

"You've no disagreement," Kirstine called out. "Lachlann, desist."

He ignored her. "Drop your weapon."

She appealed to Egann. "Stop this."

"Yon knight can stop it by dropping that axe. A nasty-looking piece," he added with grudging admiration.

Lachie paused just out of reach of a full swing of the gleaming axe. "Does that weapon of yours have a name?"

"None that you need know."

Lachie spun his sword so the blade sung in the night air. "This is Dread-Mordad, and it is pleased to meet you."

"I'm glad to know what to call it when I claim it from you."

"Last chance," Lachie warned.

"Please do as they say," she called to the knight, who could have no idea of Lachie's deadly skills. He was no ill-armed villager on the wrong side of too much ale. "Please!"

The knight's attention was diverted to Kirstine for only a moment. Lachie took advantage of it, bringing his sword up with his left hand this time. That he used both hands equally often surprised opponents. Kirstine had heard Dread-Mordad whistle through the air when Lachie was at practice, and it whistled now toward the arm holding the knight's shield.

She expected the knight to stagger, fall to one knee, and surrender. That did not happen. Instead, the blow skidded along the shield's surface, accompanied by another laugh sure to make Lachie even angrier.

Ping and shriek, clang and clatter, sword on armor on axe on shield. Her voice too tight to do more than gasp, she tried to tell Egann again to stop them, but he stood transfixed at the spectacle of Lachlann the Beardless, the

Fairhair Galrandel, matched blow for blow by an unknown knight.

The knight no longer laughed. Kirstine saw only grim intent in the clean-shaved face behind the helm — an intent equal to Lachie's. Helplessness threatened to choke her. There was no victory in this, only senseless waste.

Lachie stumbled back from a hard strike from the broadside of the knight's axe and nearly fell. She could not afford to lose him. Nor this knight, who had come to a Green Woman's aid. Gallant and powerful, clearly a better ally than enemy.

There was a burning in her bodice as her heart pounded. As with the harp last night, she suddenly felt held up by chanting voices. The words were foreign, yet she understood.

Are these not your lands? Is their blood not your blood?

Indeed, she realized. Why did she expect someone other than her to intercede?

A wave of calm rose inside her. She began to urge her mare toward the combatants, but something touched her knee. With a gasp she saw that Breda was offering her a hefty bucket of water.

With a laugh of her own, Kirstine seized the handle, urged her mare again toward the fight, stood in the stirrups, and flung the contents over both combatants. She tossed the heavy bucket at Lachie's head for good measure.

PART TWO

Skyra of Stane

Chapter Eight

"Fools with sharp knives. Not everything is meat for your carving!"

Skyra's opponent deflected Breda's well bucket toward her and she danced out of the way. Shaking water out of her eyes and about to shout an insult at the water thrower still astride their mount, she gawked instead at the hair that glowed with firelight. Those were graceful hands at the reins of the lathered mare.

Her battle fury blew away like ash, and she took a step back to signal an end to her desire to fight.

Her opponent, tall as her and lean, and no less able for a foreshortened arm, rushed her. Caught off her guard, she was knocked onto her back. She returned his lack of courtesy with a knee to the inside of his thigh, precious close to his future progeny. It succeeded in robbing his breath for a moment, and she shoved him to one side. She grabbed up her axe as she rolled to her feet and found herself facing him again.

"Lachlann, stop!" The lady wheeled her mare between them. "You're only upset because this knight's done our work for us."

One of the pitchfork bearers ran for the wood. A soldier gave chase on his horse, catching the runner by his collar and knocking him down. He cried out as he tumbled over his pitchfork, and Breda, who was already tending the wounded man Skyra had first felled, shouted in her thick voice, "Could you stop hurting each other for one blessed minute?"

Slowly, her gaze on her opponent, Skyra lowered her axe to set the heel lightly on the ground next to her foot. He mirrored her after a moment, took a step back, and touched the point of his sword to the ground in front of him.

"They had it coming to them, didn't they?" Quickly, Skyra added, "I'm sorry, Breda. I don't know any of these men. Mayhap my being here brought this on us."

The woman, still astride her mare, said firmly, "They're here because of ewes that died in the flooding."

"Truly?" Then she was glad she'd knocked each of them on their backside at least once. She hadn't meant to strike the man with the gashed arm so hard, but they'd set fire to the drying hut and the smoke of that obnoxious plant had made her sneeze just as she struck him.

The woman cocked her head. "Yes, truly. They were overheard."

"That I believe. They've been taking turns lurking in the wood. They were loud." She fanned her face as she added, "Loud and fragrant."

"You were ready for them."

"Fools are predictable. I knew they'd come tonight with the moon not yet risen." Skyra started when her opponent, the man called Lachlann, turned abruptly, but it was toward Breda to offer his aid. He moved like a hungry cat, and that trick of his using his sword in either hand was enviable.

He meant Breda no harm, so she returned her attention to the lady. In the dimming flame of the fire and wreathed in its smoke, her face shone like the moon. Skyra blinked her eyes to fend off a rising sensation of beguilement.

"May I know your name?"

All at once she was suspicious of the lady's sweetness. "Tell me yours and I'll tell you mine."

Breda's voice was heavy with warning. "She is Lady Kirstine of Castle Drummoch." The scolding tone faded as she added, "I'm glad to see you are well, Lady."

"Your care and advice have sustained me."

Skyra saw in their shared glance that more was said than the words.

Breda tipped her head toward Lachlann as he knelt next to her, holding fresh cloth as Breda bound it to the man's arm. "And you, good sir. I've not forgotten our wild ride."

"Nor I." They laughed at a shared memory and the tension drained out of Skyra's shoulders. These were truly friends, and she need not fear for Breda in their company.

She realized that Lady Kirstine was regarding her from eyes very dark in one so fair of hair. Whoever this local lady might be, her soldiers were well-trained and efficient. Skyra was grateful to have crossed swords with this Lachlann and not been injured. From the silhouette of both their faces, she also reckoned Lady Kirstine and Lachlann were related. They shared high brows, wide-set eyes, narrow noses, and generous mouths, but his clean-shaved face bore no sign of the dimples that flashed when the lady smiled.

"Lady Kirstine." She bowed her head in genuine respect. "I am Skyra of Stane."

"Stane? Where is that?"

She was spared answering that she had no idea when they were interrupted by the dark-of-face and heavy-of-beard man whose armor showed a mark of rank. He'd been having a quiet, pointed conversation with his captives. "The night deepens. What would you have done with them, Lady?"

With a fluid sweep of her heavy, well-made cloak, Lady Kirstine dismounted. She was tall, though not as tall as Skyra, and her cloak fell from her level shoulders without break to the ground. Slender, then, and graceful, with a voice cool and steady like a deep mountain stream.

Lachlann left off helping Breda, who was nearly done anyway, and rose to his feet to support the lady's arm, though Skyra could see no reason the lady couldn't walk unassisted.

He said none too quietly to her, "Androw would have ordered public whipping."

The captives groaned even as the lady recoiled. "What good is that to Breda? What does that teach them?"

"It teaches them a lesson about committing violence on unarmed women."

Skyra thought it was likely not the right moment to point out that she was, in fact, armed.

"What does a violent lesson teach? That violence is permissible if you have the power to be violent? Which is what all of them thought when they came here, that having enough power to set a fire and attack a woman was permission to do so." Lady Kirstine patted his hand on her arm before pushing off his grasp. With a light step, she closed the distance between her and the circle of captives.

Skyra knelt to wipe her axe edges on a clump of grass. The light from the hut fire was fading as the flames sank into a dank smolder. Helping Breda clear away brush in the weeks past had seemed a thankless chore, but now the need for it was abundantly clear. The attackers had chosen badly for the fire — the sweet chervil inside was still thickly wet. After the thin roof and walls had burned there was little left to catch flame.

She stifled another sneeze as she rose. Water from the bucket dousing trickled down her back, a sensation she hated.

Breda had assured herself that the man who had tripped on his pitchfork was uninjured and retreated to the door of the cottage, holding herself apart from any judgment. It was her goddess's way, Skyra knew. Taking up position between Breda and the cluster of prisoners, horses, and soldiers, she watched Lady Kirstine stop in front of each man until they looked up. She held their gaze for three or four heartbeats before moving on, taking their measure.

Headache lanced behind Skyra's eyes, and she stifled a whimper. She had seen this done before. Smoke in the air, cries of the wounded, hundreds herded by horse and rope to the center of the field. The order then had been decimation, one random man in ten put to the sword or axe. Her arm ached anew from the bloody work—

She did not want this memory. She was no longer there, and no matter how she tried, she could not put a name or time to that place.

Lady Kirstine had stepped back, hands on her hips. "You have caused harm this night, and I assign to you all a penance. Each of you will return tomorrow at daylight and each day after until the hut is rebuilt and restocked as Breda wishes."

Exceedingly fair, Skyra thought, and would spare her being the one to do it on her own. The lady was not done, however.

"When that work is complete, good Breda will teach you how to find and dry the healing herb that grows lochside, and how to make it into the ointment that eases udder rot in all manner of animals. For these lessons you shall bring your eldest son or daughter with you, so that they may also benefit from good Breda's wisdom. They will care well for their own flocks ever after. Do you swear to undertake this penance?"

Three of the men immediately said yes, and the fourth quickly after. The coward who had seemed in charge but had let his less sturdy comrades challenge Skyra first finally agreed, but with clear ill-grace.

Lachlann scoffed, however. "They'll not do it unless forced."

"One of the men can stay here until it's done," the heavy-bearded captain offered.

"I have no need of that," Breda called. "These good men will keep their word."

"I will make sure it's done," Skyra said, surprising herself. For a moment the stars seemed bright as the sun, and she quelled the urge to shake her head free of dizziness.

Lady Kirstine's smile, wide and genuine, eased Skyra's headache. "I thank you, knight of Stane." To the man with the slashed arm she added, "I'm sure good Breda will continue to see to your wounds as well, and lucky you are for her kind soul."

"Lady," the captain said carefully, "I don't doubt that this soldier can see your word is done, but I'll billet a man in the village to encourage them to return on the morrow. Unless yon knight has a horse, it will be a long walk to roust them all."

At the lady's inquiring glance, Skyra acknowledged, "There is no horse here."

"I think that's wise, Egann." Lady Kirstine added, "I understand that whippings might be faster, but they fix nothing, and don't make Breda safer. If they know and learn from her, they should no longer fear her. It is wisdom she offers, not sorcery." Her voice took on an edge of menace as she stared down at the coward. "If you fail in your share of this penance, a whipping is so ordered."

"Understood." Captain Egann nudged the foot of the nearest prisoner. "Count yourselves lucky that Fair and Wise Kirstine was your judge tonight. I've not near so generous a heart."

"Nor I," Lachlann echoed.

The captain turned back to the lady. "We'll set them to dumping water on the fire. When it's out, we'll walk them back to the village and then return to escort you home."

"I don't like leaving her alone." Skyra didn't miss the suspicious look Lachlann aimed at her when he spoke.

As she drew off her heavy iron-woven gloves, the scales of her vambraces grated on one another. She'd not oiled them enough, clearly. As when she recalled her name, the ritual language of the moment came to her as natural as breathing. "Of course I will pledge myself to the lady's safety during your absence, by whatever oath you require."

"Lachlann, this good knight means me no harm." Kirstine's voice grew amused. "You must admit, the protection offered is near equal to your own. I can always throw a bucket."

"It's a good thing you missed me," he retorted.

"I never intended to hit you with it." The flutter of her dark lashes put the lie to her words.

Skyra didn't know what else he might have said. The crease in her helm was awakening the lingering bruise on the side of her head. That's why she felt dizzy, she reasoned. Danger was past, so she pulled it off and let her braids and loose hair fall free. "Only men need fear me."

Everyone stopped talking. Then the silence was broken by the high, clear bells of Lady Kirstine's delighted laughter.

For a moment so brief that even the stars had not time to flicker, Skyra rose out of herself on the curl of that beautiful sound as it soared above the trees. The edge of the rising moon broke over the horizon. Not-memory came, for she was certain that she had never in this life felt magic so close to her. Night magic, star magic, made of wonder and shadows and light.

Not a memory. She was called to her future.

Chapter Nine

"How did you get here?"

Once the lady's mare had been watered, Breda had made the three of them hot tea and they sat at the long table. Skyra was glad of the warmth. Under her armor she was wet where the water from the bucket had seeped and growing chilled as the iron cooled with the night air. Lady Kirstine had her hands wrapped around the mug and was holding it to her face to breathe in the steam.

"I walked."

"Truly?" Lady Kirstine didn't hide her skepticism. "Breda knows nothing of your clan. I recognize not any element of your armor save the spiral seals. I think they may be mere decoration and not a sigil of service. Yet you speak this language as my husband does."

Skyra grunted. "I have no idea how your husband speaks."

Kirstine asked her something, but in another tongue. At Skyra's shake of the head, she said, "That's Galrandic."

"I've no memory of hearing it before."

Breda pushed a shallow dish toward the center of the table. "If I had to guess, I'd say she's got more of the northern ice in her than even I do. Vestfold or farther."

Skyra's mouth watered as she inhaled the sharp aroma of roasted chestnuts mashed in the fresh, tangy cheese Breda made from the goat's milk. Kirstine wasted no time smearing some of the cheese on a wedge of barley hardtack that had been soaking for a few minutes in the light ale one of the villagers regularly brought Breda. Having heard the lady's stomach growling earlier, Skyra guessed she'd not had supper.

"Bless your table, Breda. Thank you." Kirstine ate the cracker in two bites and reached to make another. "We need to keep more goats at the castle. This is as delicious as it is fortifying."

"Goats eat nearly anything and give us this wonder. The goddess provides." Breda sighed. "I am glad that they didn't hurt my animals. After Beltane, I'll graze them in sweet clover. The cheese from that milk is the best of the year."

After another warming swallow of the hot tea, Skyra asked, "If I am from places more north than here, where are you from, Lady?"

"Across the ocean and to the south, in warmer climes. My Galrandel people are of the Fairhair, who lived in those lands long ago."

Fairhair. The lady's hair was indeed like moonlight around her pale face. The thick, single braid, coiled and pinned to the top of her head, was the white gold of late summer hay. Eyes that had seemed only dark and watchful shone now with amber depths in Breda's lamplight, and Skyra made herself look away.

Kirstine finished her second cracker and took up her tea. "So you were injured, but you know not where, and you walked here on a path you also don't recall?"

"That's the truth of it. My head still aches." Skyra reached for Breda's dull cheese knife and spread a cracker for herself.

"I should tell you that I know when people are lying."

"It's not a lie." Skyra scowled at the idea.

"It's not the entire truth."

She had nothing more to say to that. As beguiling as Lady Kirstine was, she had not earned being privy to Skyra's imaginings. The night's events had shaken something in her, but this lady didn't need to know that either.

"You know your name is Skyra of Stane."

"It came to me all in a flash. There are moments of memory, but as if from the other side of a wall in an already dark room."

Kirstine licked a smear of cheese off her thumb before asking, "And you truly don't know where Stane is?"

Skyra saw no reason to repeat herself.

The golden dark eyes shone with a sudden humor. "I'm going to have to drag every answer out of you, aren't I?"

"As you like."

The look she got then stole her breath. It was teasing, almost a dare, as if the anticipation of a battle with words was a delightful prospect and the lady often lacked a quality combatant.

Breda had risen to go to her herb cabinet and returned with a twist of hay and sage in her strong hand. "Your head hurts, I can tell."

"I don't need that," Skyra protested. Her throat half closed at the memory of the last dosing.

Lady Kirstine regarded her over the top of her mug. "Why are you choosing to be in pain?"

"I'm measuring the pain against the taste."

Breda set the curative on the table in front of Skyra. "My bee syrup is for the young ones, not grown women."

"It can't be that bad." So quickly that Skyra was startled, Kirstine drew a short dagger, likely from her boot, and cut a quarter of the twist away. With an easy twirl, the dagger returned under the table. She put the portion of the curative in her mouth with a thoughtful look.

Skyra had been wrong to think this lady's only defenses were her dignity and charm. She crossed her arms over her chest and waited.

After a few chews, Kirstine delicately spat the concoction into her hand. "I agree that there is a level of pain I'd keep to avoid this."

Breda narrowed her eyes when Skyra laughed. "Live with your aching head, then. It might ease if you got out of that armor and wet leathers."

Skyra agreed, but she felt in need of its protection, though why was a puzzle. "I'm fine."

"You're straining my bench every time you move. Come on."

As Breda made to get up, Kirstine waved her back into place. "Rest easy. You've had a worrisome night. I've long helped with my brother's and husband's armor, and that of my sons."

Skyra lifted her arms and swept her hair up so that Kirstine could reach the ties that bound the breastplate to the chain mail back. It was easier when someone helped, this was true. She was acutely aware of the hint of lavender that clung to the lady's clothes. "Lachlann — is that your brother?"

"Yes. To be truthful, we share only our father."

She felt the first few ties on her side loosen. "If you unfasten the ones over my shoulder, I can lift it off."

"And take your ears with it. Patience, please." There was light mocking in her tone, as she would use with kin or a child. Skyra felt her face grow hot and averted it farther from the lady's quick eyes. She was holding her breath, she realized, and forced herself to relax.

"These rings, for the bindings — I've not seen them before. Drummoch armor has hooks. These are much quicker."

"Rings don't slip the tether." Skyra spoke it as fact, though she couldn't have said why she knew it so firmly. Kirstine was standing behind her and finally unfastening the ties at her shoulders. There was a whisper of Kirstine's breath on her neck.

Memory came as gently as that breath, settling on her like a sweet-scented breeze. The skin across her neck and chest tightened in response. Another woman, standing behind her and running her hands under the heavy plate to find her breasts. The tickle of fingers and laughter. The tenderness of a woman's lips at her nape, across her temples, and on her mouth. Her head filled with the music of sighs.

A hundred shivers, all at once, shook through her as she clutched the loosened breastplate to her chest. The leather jerkin under it and her undershirt were both damp. She was chilled — that was why her nipples ached. Too easily she could picture Kirstine's long and supple fingers warming them.

The sound of hooves approaching at a leisurely canter shook her out of her stupor. Kirstine set the chain mail on the cot next to Skyra's helm and went to the door. "No doubt it's Lachlann returned."

Skyra quickly pulled on the ties of the hip covers and shook down the mail around each leg. While Lady Kirstine's back was to her, she donned the man's trousers Breda had found for her and yanked a dry jerkin over her head. "I'll see if his horse needs watering."

Kirstine let her pass and she welcomed the smolder of the fire to mask the lingering scent of the lady's lavender. She sneezed and felt both clearer of head and dizzier.

Lachlann had dismounted by the time she reached him.

"Let me uncover the trough. I didn't want ash to get into the rainwater."

He hesitated, then nodded as he loosened the bridle and slipped the bit from the gray's mouth. "I appreciate that. The village is thin with food, and the others made do. I hoped to find something for my horse here."

He said nothing of his own hunger, even though Skyra suspected that, like his sister, he'd not had an evening meal either. "There's dried fodder Breda keeps for wounded animals. Your sister's mare ate it without trouble. At this point it's mostly hay, but there's dried apple and chestnut mash in it too."

"That'll do." He thumped his tall stallion's flank and spoke to it with an uncomplicated, boyish affection. "There's a real rubdown waiting at home for you, Greylach. You've enjoyed yourself, haven't you?"

She did as promised and found herself having much the same conversation as she'd had with his sister. He, too, had never heard of Stane.

"Are you certain of it?"

"I am."

"Where were you struck?"

She used the edge of her hand to show him the angle from temple to the bone behind her ear.

"I've seen men lie senseless for days from a blow like that," he acknowledged.

"I apparently got up and walked. For a very long way."

He'd drawn a small curry brush from his saddlebag and was lightly combing it across his horse's flanks. More to refresh the horse for the ride home than to do any real cleaning, Skyra knew, just as she'd done with Lady Kirstine's mare. Seeing to the mare had given the lady and Breda a chance to talk privately, and it had put off the inevitable interrogation.

This Lachlann had the same manner about him that his sister did — at least when not angered. He asked when another noble-born might have ordered, and he showed gratitude for small favors.

"Might you have crossed on a vessel from the Norse kingdom?"

She shrugged. "It's possible I did, but I don't know who would have taken me aboard. I was a bloody mess when I arrived here."

"Mayhap they thought you might be useful aboard ship."

"I doubt that I was. I don't know the knots."

He stopped to stare at her for a moment. "Curious."

"It is. I don't know why they wouldn't have thrown me overboard or taken my armor from me."

"Though you don't remember, I doubt that you would have allowed that without a fight. Mayhap that was new blood on top of old injuries. That head bruise might be a new injury from someone who tried to rob you."

That hadn't occurred to her. She'd assumed she'd staggered here fresh from the large battle that tickled the edges of her memory. Was that not the way it had happened?

His tone growing troubled, he said, "Mayhap you were a hiresword and far from home to follow work."

"Mayhap," she echoed quietly. "I wish I knew."

She heard the door of the cottage open and close. The quick, light footsteps told her it was Kirstine, not Breda. She carried a small bowl and Skyra smelled the goat's cheese.

"You must be hungry. I certainly was."

He tucked the brush away and took the bowl from his sister with thanks. Mouth near full, he managed, "Why don't we have more of this at home?"

"Androw prefers sheep's cheese, or cow's."

Brother gave sister a droll look. "Androw is on his way to the other side of the world."

Kirstine's smile widened. "I was thinking to add a few more goats to the near pasture and see what cook can make of the milk."

"I support you in that, dear sister. This tastes of home. Can you be ready to go soon?" He handed back the empty bowl.

"Let me take my leave of Breda."

Skyra made herself not watch Kirstine as she ducked her head to pass under the lintel of the cottage door. "I gave the lady's mare a light rub."

"Horses and women, a little affection makes both easy..." He cleared his throat. "Stable talk," he muttered.

"I'm sure I've heard plenty of such."

"Did you billet with men? Or were there more of you?" He added with good humor, "I confess that thought fills me with terror."

That was a question she'd asked herself. "I am not certain. My instinct is that I was in a large company of men at some point. When you and I sparred, it felt familiar, as when I practice every morning. I know it without knowing how." Mayhap she'd shared quarters with men as soldiers. She knew now that she'd shared intimacies with women — and the thought of such no sooner crossed her mind than her arms and hips grew heavy with the misted memory of passionate hours.

Kirstine and Breda emerged from the cottage, laughing together about something. Skyra fetched the lady's mare and stepped back as Kirstine set the bit and tightened the bridle. She stroked the mare's neck with a calming hum. "Shall we go home, my girl?"

Though Kirstine was not speaking to her, Skyra answered, "Yes," in her mind. The answer was yes.

Without thinking on the wisdom of it, she dropped to one knee and offered her laced fingers to help the lady mount. It was no effort to lift her.

With a ruffle of her cloak, Kirstine was safely in her saddle. "Thank you, good knight. Very gallant, don't you think, Lachlann?"

Skyra's brain was spinning with the idea of how simple it would be to carry this lady to bed, to smell her secrets and swim in her pleasures. Let it not show on my face, she prayed. "I doubt that I am a knight. Your brother suggests that mayhap I am a hiresword."

"For your effort this night in protection of the weak, you could be a sworn knight." Looking down, her bright hair not yet covered by the hood, Kirstine's dark eyes glimmered with starfire. "It was a blessing that you were here."

"Fortune was indeed kind." Lachlann gigged his gray toward the path. "I know not your future plans but hope that they have adventure and honor."

With a flick of one wrist, Lady Kirstine circled her mare to follow him. "If you find you are no longer a blessing here, may you discover better use for your skills."

"I will endeavor to make it so."

The lady might have asked what she meant, but her brother called to her. Skyra watched them disappear into the shadowed moonlight.

Chapter Ten

Breda surveyed the rebuilt drying hut with approval. "You've done well, all."

Equally pleased as Breda was, Skyra tempered her habitual scowl with an attempt at a smile. "You've surely done a better job with this roof than I did with the one on the cottage."

Railbert, a jovial man who'd admitted his part in the venture had been much spurred by drink and the idea of an early Beltane bonfire, bowed lavishly to Breda. "About that roof, good woman. Would you be up for a barter to see it done properly?"

"I would. Shall we discuss it?" Breda gestured at the log-made bench that was a twin to the one Skyra was perched on.

Enjoying the warming sun of midday, Skyra resettled her attention on the remaining men. Only the coward had been trouble, but not for long. As with knowing the fit of her armor, she knew his type. Men like him were always angry and always looking for a place to pour that anger. Even his own anger made him angry, like a leaf in a whirlpool of its own making. Breda's gentle and steady kindness had soothed him, for now. He would lash out again, but Skyra was near convinced that it would not be at Breda.

What more could she do to make Breda safe? Lady Kirstine's parting words, *If you find you are no longer a blessing here*, played again in her mind. Though Breda had said nothing, she was largely healed in body, if not mind. Last night's events felt as if she had been here for a reason. Now that reason was past.

The idea that she had forgotten a life not only as a soldier, but also as a hiresword, was perplexing, to be sure. But she couldn't reject the idea. Mulling over it had troubled her sleep.

The puzzle of her past was not the only thing that had kept her awake, though, and she knew it. She had let her mind drift to the misty memory of women, and of knowing intimacy with them. Her body had warmed and softened, and her mind filled with the promise of future pleasure in the same way that today's sun on her face was the promise of summer at last.

She had been unable to keep Lady Kirstine out of her dreams. She'd awoken twice with the lady's smile in her eyes. This was desire, she knew that now, and this desire was not a stranger. Her mind dwelt on the supple hands and soft lips, and on the grace that so lightly mounted a horse. There was more than that, however. The hands were gentle, the lips spoke with wit, and there was a different grace in how she had treated the men at her mercy last night. Instinct said Skyra had not known such qualities in a lady before. Training whispered that such knowledge could be dangerous.

The afternoon passed quickly as she and Breda led the work party farther afield to find more sweet chervil to fill the rebuilt hut. Skyra's sneezing nose proved very helpful, much to her dismay. By the time the men left to walk to their homes, they were eagerly promising to return for the lesson Lady Kirstine had also ordered.

Throughout their supper, Skyra pondered the question she wanted to ask Breda but feared would give away her inner turmoil. Finally, as they worked near the fire, she could resist no longer. "What did you make of the two Fairhair last night?"

"I think they have known light." The prominent, stiff knuckles on Breda's hands didn't slow their rippling movement across the small loom. "But I felt a darkening near them. A shadow that crosses the goddess's goodwill."

After the lady and her brother had departed, Breda had spent much time staring into the fire as she sipped a foul-smelling tea made from a dried and crushed mushroom. Skyra knew nothing of such traveling in one's mind. "Did you see that in your wandering last night?"

"I saw a change of tide and rising water. A boat of light against a dark wind."

Though she wasn't convinced Breda's tea offered more than dreams while awake, she was alarmed. "Is she in danger? Does something hunt her?"

Breda gave her a sharp look. "Tomorrow hunts for us all."

"Tomorrow." She recalled the vision of night and star magic brought on by the lady's delighted, wondrous laughter. "I don't know my past. But I feel a future calling me."

"Go on Beltane, near three weeks hence," Breda said quietly. "The auspices are always good on Beltane."

The fire crackled for a time.

"I will miss you," Skyra was finally able to say.

"And I you. I don't believe we'll meet again, but I'm not always right about these things."

She swallowed down the lump in her throat. "Now you tell me this, when I've taken every word as from your goddess herself?"

Though Breda pursed her lips, she only said, "I wish you knew her better. She asks nothing of you but to know her."

"I fear I lack the peace to hear her voice." It was true; she had no patience for a studying ritual.

"You could take the tea. A small amount to let your mind slip the bridle of your body and this place as you sleep. I have wondered if it would shake the walls of your memory."

Skyra thought to reject the idea out of hand. She had no wish to dream walk or do whatever it was that Breda experienced when she communed with her goddess. Nevertheless, it was true she was locked out from places in her own mind. There was much she was sure she could tell herself. "A small amount?"

"No more than a sip. I use it on those hurt who need to escape from their pain, and none have been harmed."

Her trust in Breda was true, and she gave a terse nod. "I will try it, then."

"I can't promise that what you might see won't be confusing or frightening. Such visions are not predictable. But you will wake in the morning refreshed." The older woman set aside the loom and went to her cupboard of curatives.

The grate of the pestle against Breda's grinding stone brought Skyra to her feet. She readied the warm rocks for their beds and set her axe and shield near her cot where she would find them quickly. Clad in the too-small nightshirt, she felt like a child as Breda brought her the hot drink.

The sip was bitter, and she felt nothing but its warmth down her throat and through her chest. After she had made herself comfortable and Breda had put out the lamp, she thought the warmth had extended into her gut, then lower still.

With the heat came the thought of Lady Kirstine. The moonlight of her hair surrounded Skyra's bed, bringing with it the softness of feathery clouds in summer skies.

Her bones unknitted, first her shoulders, then her chest. All the sharp edges were dissolved, and she was poured out, molten. The flicker of fire and knell of heavy hammers shook the bed, nearly waking her. Her mind cried out for purpose, and it was given, firm and clear.

Her thoughts were a silver bird in full flight, rising to the sun. Golden bells of laughter trembled in the sky. A chorus of women rose in battle cry and victorious song. She drifted toward the calling to her soul, wishing to take in the words, but they made no sense.

These are not my memories.

A blood-red dagger slit the sky and grief poured in. The song was all loss and terror. A boat of light sailed to ruin against a dark wind. Loneliness, an echo of her own. She had lost her kin, her place, and her purpose too.

Spirit in pieces, she fumbled against a wall she could not see, palms seeking an opening. Finally her fingertips sensed a softening, and she pushed at it. A sliver of light near blinded her, and she covered her face with her hands.

Her fingers glowed orange against her eyes. When the light seemed at last to grow no brighter, she cautiously lowered them to find that a door in the dark had opened. She could see through it for only a moment, then she was in the room beyond and cradled in strong arms. Walls of burnished log rose around her, and a bright fire in a stone fireplace was so warm she thought her eyebrows might melt. Her small hands reached for cake offered by a woman with braids like hers. Fruit and dark sugars exploded in her mouth.

She was completely happy, though a howling wind drove ice pellets against the tightly shuttered windows. The arms that held her were like iron in their safety, and a low, rumbling voice sang into the dark night. These words she knew. He sang in solemn prayer for the raven to circle through the forest and turn time and the seasons to spring.

Who am I?

Sky, the answer came. *Sky and rain. Soldier and sword. Rider and horse. Ruin and ruin and ruin...*

These were not answers. *Who am I?*

::You already know.::

There is more to me than a winter solstice memory.

She closed her eyes to the past and saw Kirstine again, her hair spread out on white linens and beckoning in her eyes. Purpose, firm and clear.

She woke drenched in sweat, but without other ill effects. The rocks at her feet still gave off warmth. The familiar cadence of Breda's snores was reassuring.

It was only a dream, she told herself. There was no invitation in the lady's eyes.

Though she hadn't believed Breda's tea would fix her broken memory, she was disappointed, nevertheless. She'd learned that she had once been a child, like everyone else, and that was all.

I was a happy child, she amended. *I was a happy child who knew what love was.* She smiled in the dark at the taste of the fruited cake in her mouth. It amazed her that something so simple and long ago could bring such certainty of joy in an innocent world.

Sleep, easy and normal, gently claimed her. She pictured once again Kirstine's fine features and dark eyes and relived the moment when she'd knelt at the lady's feet to help her mount. How could this woman be her purpose? To what end? Honor? Or ruin?

There was no way to know but to go.

At sunrise on Beltane, with Breda's blessing, she went.

Chapter Eleven

Skyra resettled the ungainly sack over her right shoulder, which wearied from its weight. She wore her leathers for the long walk. Her boots had been repaired as best as Breda could manage, and she hoped they lasted the distance to Castle Drummoch.

The sack holding her armor, and small items Breda had pressed on her, clanked with every step. She planned to stop when she knew the castle was near and put on at least the breastplate and back. Her axe, riding over her left shoulder, told its own story, this was true, but if she hoped to be taken into the captain's company, she had best look more like a soldier.

Mayhap they would send her away, not wanting a woman in their ranks. If so, she didn't know what she would do. There only hope to fuel the long walk, and she clung to it even as she called herself a likely fool and schooled herself for disappointment.

The morning was all the wonder of spring. Rainbows glistened in the runoff-fed waterfalls on the hills above her. In every cluster of homes and markets, no matter how small, there was a nearby field with stacks of wood ready for the twin bonfires. Doors and gates were hung with yellow buds and greenery. Children chased each other across the bonfire fields in carefree abandon. She delighted to see the signs of holiday, but now she wondered about Breda's claim of good auspices. What were the chances she'd find the captain in the castle when there would be, no doubt, a festival crowd in the town nearby to keep under control?

The sun had only just reached its full height when she came in sight of Castle Drummoch and the long inlet from the sea beyond it. High on a cliff, the keep seemed to be half carved out of gray rock, and the curtain wall that enclosed the bailey was as tall as two men. It was not as large as... As...

The name would not come to her, and she put the frustration away. Best to face forward toward her future, whatever it may be.

Columns of gray smoke inside the curtain wall were sufficient for both a kitchen and forge at work. Outside the curtain wall, and down a long incline from the castle, the town of Drummbhaile was centered at the intersection of three bustling roads. The west and east roads, like the northerly one she walked, were a sprawl of cottages and small pastures green with new grass and separated with fences of stacked stones or the jagged gray teeth of rocks too large to move.

The curl of another forge on the far outskirts indicated smithcraft beyond that of the castle's needs. If she should find a way to earn coin, she'd have the remaining dent in her helm hammered out and acquire a decent pair of hose to go with new boots.

Her stomach had long since finished the breakfast of pottage and eggs Breda had made for her. Under the shelter of an old oak with only the first buds of spring leaves on its lower branches, she unwrapped hardtack and cheese and enjoyed the sun as she ate. Once the grumbles of her stomach were quelled, she put on her upper body armor and laced the vambraces to her forearms. She left her hair free as she pulled on her helm, hoping it would call her easily to the captain's memory.

Strangely hopeful, for she had no reason to be, she rejoined the other foot travelers on the road. The crowd was thickening with families and friends singing snatches of song and raucously blowing pipes.

The brief rest had eased the tenderness in her feet. She was glad of that as she strove for a steady marching pace up the steep, rutted incline to the thick castle gate. The two well-armored guards who flanked it were clearly taking her measure.

"Hold and state your business," the taller one called when she was yet a few steps from him.

"I wish a few words with Captain Egann, or Lachlann, brother to Lady Drummoch."

"Why would they want words with you?"

"I offer service."

The round guard openly scoffed from behind his broad and bushy beard. "What service would that be, woman?"

"They know me as a fighter," she explained, striving to keep her tone helpful. She turned her palms upward to indicate her armor.

The taller guard cocked his head. "Are you the Stane?"

She blinked in confusion. "I am Skyra of Stane."

"The Galrandel is in the keep, I believe. He spoke of you at ale. I did not believe him, but here you are." His bearded face twisted into what Skyra chose to take as a grin. "Quite a sight to see."

"I am very real." She resisted the urge to put her hand on the dagger in her belt to end this tiresome conversation. "How might I find him in the keep?"

"Ask in the great hall." The guard's incredulous laughter followed her as she walked resolutely toward the high doors he pointed out.

Thankfully the doors stood open, and she was able to stride through with all the dignity possible while carrying a clanking sack on her back.

The hall's shutters were all open to the warm air, and the aroma of roast food and bread wafted in on the breeze. She doffed her helm, tucking it under her shield arm, and glanced around in hope of being greeted by a steward or footman. But the vaulted chamber stood empty. Mayhap everyone was out to see the bonfires lit. It was near time.

The long hall was headed by a dais where an ornate chair was raised above all else. Doors to either side undoubtedly led deeper into the keep. As she was debating the wisdom of using one of them, the left-hand door opened and a young woman, dark of hair and eye, hurried in.

"I see it here," she called to someone behind her. She ran up the two steps to the high table on the dais and caught up a long red-and-gold wrap from under a chair.

"I don't know how I forgot it — oh!"

Lady Kirstine, her moonlight hair covered with a white coif and her arms full of greenery, froze in the doorway. The steady, dark gaze contained the luster of beckoning starlight, bidding Skyra to follow a path she could not see. "You've come."

"Yes," was all she said. The pulse of an undeniable truth brought a pounding to her temples and ringing in her ears, but she did not add, *Of course.*

PART THREE

Beltane

Chapter Twelve

Of course.

Of course she's come, Kirstine thought.

Anticipating and navigating the diplomatic dangers of High Court yesterday and supervising preparation for the rites and feast of Beltane today had consumed all of Kirstine's daylight hours for the past few weeks. At night, however, in her precious hours alone, she had allowed herself to linger on the surprising and welcome verbal sparring she'd had with the woman knight.

There had also been dreams. She would not think on them now. They confused her deeply and were full of melting, delicious promises she had no faith in.

They might be true, whispered her unruly mind. *Here she is, after all.*

"Have you come for Beltane?" was all she could think to say.

"Yes. Mayhap a while longer than that."

She is an impossibility, Kirstine thought. So tall, and utterly intriguing, from the spiral signet hammered into her breastplate, to the large, jangling sack she carried effortlessly on her back. Her burnished red hair that hung around her shoulders and the length of her back caught the sunlight in a blaze of fire. So serious, but Kirstine's dreams had been filled with the rare smiles that changed her eyes from ice to warm summer sky.

Impossible, yet here she was, walking across Kirstine's hall with the ghostings of that intriguing smile on her otherwise stern face.

"I cannot stop — the bonfires are due to be lit, and these are my offering." She pointed with her chin at the masses of weeds and clippings she'd collected from the castle garden.

Skyra stopped a few feet from her and ducked her head. "Shall I accompany you?"

"No." The reply was immediate, without thought.

"I'm sorry. I don't know your customs."

"The women go first — oh." At that she had to laugh at herself. "I forgot for a moment and saw only the soldier."

One eyebrow went up. "I am flattered. I think."

"In truth, yes, you can accompany me. Lachlann was quite cross that I wouldn't allow him with me. There are many strangers in the crowd, and women — he has learned this quite recently — can be dangerous."

Marial, who had been hovering in uncertainty, stifled a giggle.

Skyra's lips twitched and Kirstine had to look away from the fascinating sparkle of light in the now blue eyes. That light filled her dreams with warmth and something else she had no experience with.

"If you wish to walk with me, you can carry some of the greenery."

"Gladly."

"Marial, as you've most likely guessed, this is Skyra of Stane. Would you show her where to put that sack and helm, and anything else she'd like in the guardroom behind the tower door to keep them safe?"

"Yes, Lady." Marial beckoned, now not bothering to hide her amusement. "Come with me."

They were back quickly, and Kirstine wished it had taken longer. Her feelings drifted like a feather, up and down and around, from amusement to astonishment to fear. The fear surprised her, for she knew, through to her very heart, that Skyra of Stane would not ever hurt her. Yet she knew equally well that Skyra was dangerous in ways Kirstine had no experience to foresee.

She was no fool — the places in her world where women were allowed to show such strength did not include someone like Skyra. She was like a creature of ancient myth. The kirk, especially, did not like any myths but their own.

"Ready?" She thrust a good half of the greenery into Skyra's arms and stood quietly as Marial wrapped her clan tartan from shoulder to opposite hip and fastened the large clan brooch over her breast. She wished she could walk to the fires with her head uncovered and hair loose, as Galrandel women did. The coif did at least keep the narrow, beaten bronze diadem of her rank as Lord Androw's consort from rubbing a blister on the back of her head.

Women from elsewhere in the castle were entering the hall through every doorway yet leaving Kirstine a path forward. In the courtyard even more were waiting — maids and cooks, and soldier's wives and daughters. Marial and clever Una joined hands with other friends and lifted up their voices in "Hey, Merry ye Merry."

Behind her, Skyra sneezed and muttered something Kirstine was certain was foul, but then her low voice joined the song.

This magic she knows, Kirstine thought.

As all women should.

That thought, so fervent as to be a prayer, brought a smile to her face. The guards at the castle gate bowed their heads as they passed, but both stole quick glances at the merry maids. Beltane fires would burn hot tonight.

Behind her Skyra was still singing and Kirstine felt buoyed by the strength of her presence, sneezes and all.

Girls with flowers in their hair, near-mothers with a babe low in their bellies, even women Kirstine knew were devoted to the kirk — they all walked out for Beltane. The cleansing in preparation for spring could not be missed. Tonight there would be drums, fiddles, and more singing, with leaping games, dancing circles, and whispers of love.

Would Skyra stay out for the drumming? Kirstine wondered what kind of man caught her fancy, or if Skyra even knew now. A strange pang unsettled her thoughts, making it hard to stay focused on the careful walking pace she'd set down the long incline and through the village. What kind of life would she herself have if she did not recall her children or parents or any of the people she cared about? Or forgot the forests of her childhood or the first time she'd lost herself in her music? To not recall life's small joys was unimaginable.

How lonely to have forgotten love.

As the growing crowd of women swarmed toward the large paddock where the bonfires were ready, Kirstine outpaced them, as was tradition. The spongy ground was very wet, and she was glad of her thick, oiled boots.

She realized that Skyra had kept pace with her, a tall shadow at her shoulder. "It's all right," she said with a backward glance.

A low grunt was the only answer she got but the crunch of Skyra's steps ceased. Another glance back showed the woman at full attention, sunlight turning her hair into a blaze of red, the base of her axe now planted in front of her, and eyes watchfully scanning the crowd. Kirstine hoped Lachie noticed that she was as ably protected as if he were the one who stood there.

Not only with skill, a small voice added, but with devotion.

Devotion? How could that be? They were only just met. Annoyed with her own fancy, she came to a stop and bowed her head to the three men at each bonfire who stood ready with torches.

A cry went up from the crowd as the torches were thrust deep into the stacked brush, wood, and peat. Moments later, oil-soaked rushes sent furling flames to the very top of the pyres. Cheers resounded as Kirstine solemnly walked to the left-hand bonfire first and cast her bundle of greenery onto it. She retreated to Skyra for the rest. "Thank you."

Skyra, clearly fighting back a sneeze, said, "This cursed weed — truly, I thank you for getting rid of it."

"The next part's fun. You'll know what to do."

She cast the second bundle onto the right-hand bonfire and returned to the spot where she had originally stopped. After a bow to the left and another to the right, she took a deep breath, pulled her white coif back to reveal her unbound Beltane hair, picked up her skirts, and ran pell-mell on the path directly between the brightly burning blazes.

Skyra's startled gasp made her laugh, and she heard the woman give chase. The ground took on a thunder as all the women behind her surged forward.

She continued to run well past the fires, all the way to the end of the meadow where the hill rose more steeply. The shoulder-high stacked stone wall had the perfect vantage to see the fires. Reaching it, she touched both hands to its cool safety. Moments later, Skyra's hands were alongside hers.

Chest heaving, she looked up at the woman to see a flush in her cheeks. "Cleansed to my bones. I truly needed that. How about you?"

A grin that matched her own feelings flashed out, leaving Kirstine dazzled. "As did I. You are not easy to catch."

"I don't mean to be."

The smile changed, echoing a dull warning bell she felt deep inside. She'd not meant to sound as if she was challenging Skyra in some way. Or had she?

"It's safer that way and that's the truth of it."

Kirstine put her back to the cool stone and surveyed the swirling crowd. Children were twirling until they dizzied themselves. Men and women held hands and clearly made pledges. Just as water was wet, there'd be handfasting in plenty during the month ahead.

"Sister." Lachie thudded to a halt near them. "I see you've picked up a bodyguard."

"A bodyguard?" Kirstine was deeply pleased at the idea even as she protested, "The knight has not agreed to such."

Skyra, without hesitation, said, "I've not been asked."

Lachlann looked Skyra up and down with much the same animosity he'd shown when they'd crossed weapons at Breda's. "You are no knight."

"I don't rightly know for certain, but I think not. The lady is generous."

He glowered. "She is generous to a fault."

"Leave off, Lachlann." Kirstine turned her face up to the sun. It felt as if it had been a year since her nose had been warm. "You wished to have me guarded earlier, and you must admit that Skyra was wholly suitable to the moment."

"See me at supper," he ordered before stalking off.

"Aye. My lord," Skyra added belatedly before falling silent.

After a minute, as the glowing, triumphant sun began to truly kiss her cheeks with warmth, Kirstine opened her eyes to see Skyra's gaze upon her. Heat of her own making rushed to her face, and she hoped that Skyra thought it was the sun's doing.

Blinking, Skyra said, "I seem to be staying for supper."

A strange shyness stole over her, along with a fire that rose in the depths of her stomach and spread through her bones. The sensation left her both languid and taut. Her mouth watered.

She'd been in a hurry all morning and not had time to do more than beg an early sample of Beltane feast bread from the kitchen. That's what ailed her — she was hungry. Thirsty.

Which did not explain why of a sudden it was so difficult to breathe or be so certain that food and drink would not satisfy her. If she had any idea of what would, she would not think to name it, not with Skyra's gaze on her.

"Would you consider it?" Her voice trembled, at least to her own ears.

"Beltane supper? Of course. I'm not a fool."

"That's not what I meant." She reached for her usual calm but found little. "You know what I mean."

Skyra's blue eyes in the sun were ringed with silver and ice, and they burned with that same light that had illuminated Kirstine's unsettling dreams. "I don't know for certain what I am. But I know much of what I'm not. Breda's way is not mine. I must make my own future."

Kirstine took a deep breath but could find nothing to say.

Skyra's voice was low and quiet as if only they were in the world. "And I have been guided here."

Kirstine's ears filled with a thrumming — not drums but her heart — and then a singular voice sent the truth through her mind.

::*She is here for you.*::

Chapter Thirteen

Skyra was surprised to find the keep's great hall dark. She'd judged that supper would be near sunset and had followed others up the long rise to the castle bailey. After their run between the Beltane fires, Kirstine had departed the Beltane field in her brother's company, leaving Skyra to wander the town. She drew stares everywhere and tried her best not to bristle.

What was left of the sunlight hardly made it the past the great hall's high windows. As her eyes adjusted to the dim interior, she could see that the empty tables of earlier in the day were now occupied shoulder to shoulder. There was an expectant silence, so she found a corner to be out of the way until she could waylay a serving maid to ask for Lachlann. It was so quiet she could hear the drumming and pipes on the Beltane field.

The evening bell rang twice. As its echo died a torchbearer appeared in the courtyard doorway. Her hand immediately went to her dagger, but she relaxed as she recognized Captain Egann's dark face and prodigious beard.

His strong, deep voice rang clear. "The fires of Beltane bring us light!"

Now there were stamps of feet and the thuds of fists on the tables. Seven men, Lachlann among them, lit their own torches from the captain's and slowly circled the hall to light rushes, which were then used to set alight the tall candles on each table. As the light grew, it shone on smiling faces and platters stacked with fist-sized rolls of dark, seed-covered wheaten bread.

Captain Egann strode to the great hearth to set the wood laid there ablaze. Scarcely a minute has passed before the entire hall glowed with new light kindled from the Beltane bonfires. The kitchen door opened, and servers appeared with trays of hot food and were greeted by a rousing cheer.

Blinking to adjust her eyes to the light, Skyra realized that she had thought it odd that the villagers below the keep had had not yet begun lighting their lamps even as the sun was setting. She knew the custom of passing between the bonfires for blessing, but this ritual of light she did not.

I am from a long way away, she reminded herself. *As at Breda's, this was familiar and not home.*

The many candles on the high table were now lit, and a sparkle drew her eye to the center. It was a gem on Lady Kirstine's diadem that flashed, but it was her shining eyes and smiling lips that kept Skyra's attention.

This place was not home, but it could be, couldn't it?

She saw that Lord Lachlann's table was directly below the dais, and he sat facing the hall, his back to his sister at the high table. Skyra had not thought he meant to take supper with her, but there was a place across from him and he was clearly looking for someone.

As she approached, he gestured at the empty place. She eased into the space on the bench, leaving her axe on her back, just as most of the men had kept their swords on their person. The men on either side scooted away, one pointedly looking the other direction, and the other pointedly looking at her. His hand was disrespectfully near his crotch and her fingers itched for her dagger.

She took this all in and told Lord Lachlann with her eyes that she had seen it. His look plainly said back, "What did you expect?"

She slowly drew her dagger, made sure its long, simple blade glinted in the nearest candlelight, then set it at the top of her place, ready for the meal. The lord frowned to mask a smile — a man with as subtle a mind as his sister, and she did appreciate that.

"Thank you," she said sincerely to the stout woman who set in front of her a trencher laden with mutton in gravy, mashed turnip, and a skewer of roasted sturgeon and onion. Alongside was a thick slice of brown bread, rich with egg and studded with dried currants, and spread with a pale jam scented with precious apricot. Instead of common barley ale, her mug was half-filled with brandied wine.

She lifted her glass to her host, Lachlann, in salute. Because she knew it to be proper, but could not say how she knew, she raised her gaze to the dais where Kirstine sat and lifted her glass to the lady as well.

"Indeed," Lachlann. He seized his gilded tankard and rose to his feet. "All hail the lady of Drummoch and this bountiful feast!"

His attention distracted from her, Skyra allowed herself a long look at Kirstine, who caught sight of her brother and blushed as his table rose to their feet. She wore a supple cloak of clan red that was trimmed with thread-of-gold thistles. Her coif was now green for Beltane. Smaller clear stones in her diadem caught the light from the candles as she bowed her head in recognition of the salute. Whomever the laughing woman at the stone wall had been, it was not she who sat center of the high table.

Skyra of course stood because the others did, but everything in her wanted to kneel. That was what one did to honor one's queen. With that thought, all the uncertainties of the long walk to get here faded into the background. She was in the right place, at long last.

Kirstine's gaze settled on her long enough for Skyra to drink from her cup in her honor.

When order was restored, everyone began eating. She grabbed one of the rapidly disappearing bread rolls and tucked into her food. Lachlann would explain his will when he was ready. She found it interesting that he was the only clean-shaved man his age. Mayhap that was the fashion in his native Galrandel. Many of the younger men at his table were also clean faced, however. He drew admiring followers, and that meant he had power beyond what his sister conveyed. That Lachlann cared for his sister was plain, but Skyra didn't yet know whose interests he put first.

It took only a minor shift of her gaze to see past him to where Lady Kirstine was clearly enjoying her supper. Skyra was saving her jam-covered bread for after the mains, but Kirstine was already biting into the bread with the abandon of a child. Their gazes met and Kirstine looked guilty, then shrugged and had another large bite. Skyra hoped Kirstine didn't think she was judging her for liking the delicious bread. Pleasures in life were infrequent. To her that seemed more reason to fully revel in them as they happened.

Her mind wandered to the pleasures more private that she had sensed when Kirstine had helped remove her armor. She shook the memory away. Clearly, the wine was not to be trusted until she had more in her stomach, and that was the truth of it. Such thoughts with the lady's hands visible at the edge of her sight were dangerous. She was better than the rude rut of a fellow next to her, or at least she would like to believe so.

She kept her gaze steady on her plate until Lachlann spoke directly to her. He was sharp-eyed and her feelings for his sister — the ones that went beyond reverence — would not please him. She wasn't sure where they would lead her, but they had drawn her here. They would keep her here.

Chapter Fourteen

"Is it your intent to stay?" Lord Lachlann dusted his hands free of crumbs over his empty trencher.

She was near done with her meal, save for a portion of the sweet bread she wanted to enjoy with the final sips of the potent wine that was easing the ache in her feet. She swallowed hastily to answer. "If I can find means to."

"You still remember nothing?"

"Nothing of value to me. Or you."

He studied her again. She returned the scrutiny.

With care to his words, he explained. "My lord Androw charged me with my sister's safety on her wedding day. I was knighted in the clan for that service. Captain Egann runs the guard, and I am happy to assist in its leadership."

She nodded her understanding and was also aware that conversation near them had ceased. Every word spoken would be carried elsewhere, just as the story of that night at Breda's had spread. The scrutiny of so many made the back of her neck itch.

He continued. "You may appeal to him for a place in the guard."

"But you believe it unlikely that he will accept me."

"Your axe he would welcome. The rest of you is too rare for his purposes."

She didn't care for that answer, but it wasn't in her power to change it. "Am I too rare for *your* purposes?"

The rude man next to her snickered but left off at Lachlann's narrow-eyed warning.

"You are rare enough to be what I didn't know was lacking. Kirst— Lady Kirstine has always been protected by the guards in Lord Androw's antechamber who took shifts at the top of the stairs. This absence of his is unprecedented for its length. When gone for a week or two we simply changed the rotation of guards. Lord Androw will be gone a year or longer."

A serving girl paused to offer him more wine, which he accepted. After a large swallow and approving grunt, he continued. "She has refused to allow me to permanently station men there, pleading the virtue of her young maid. I understand her fear and weariness of gossip." He paused for another swallow from his tankard. "Yet I am not happy that there is no weapon between the stair and her bedchamber should anyone slip past my own guards, or in my absence."

"So I might meet her approval? As a night guard?" It was less than her capabilities and the lord knew it. Nevertheless, she knew she would agree to the posting.

With every minute she grew more certain that this was the path forward in her life she was called to take.

Of course.

"Something like. A bodyguard, as required." Though he'd partaken of twice the wine she had, his gaze was steady and alert as he glanced around the room. "If she will listen to reason."

She allowed herself a glance over his head at the high table. Kirstine, her manner polite and measured, was conversing with the woman on her right. Her gaze flicked to Skyra without change in expression.

Lachlann watched as Skyra finished her sweet bread and jam. "Were you going back to the Beltane field for the drumming?"

She answered him with a shake of her head, hoping it would appear that she'd thought that far ahead. He didn't need to know she was living minute to minute and half holding her breath.

"Come with me, then."

She gulped down the last of the wine. Her dagger she returned to her belt, the tip of it passing an inch closer than good manners to her loutish neighbor's arm.

"Careful there," the lout protested.

"I am always careful."

Skyra was aware of Kirstine's bright and curious gaze on them as Lachlann led her through the door behind and left of the high table. Skyra glanced side to side in the long corridor. The smell of the kitchen was stronger here, along with the rushes on the stone floor. Directly across was a narrow door flanked by two alert guards who looked enviously toward the dining hall. Lachlann greeted them and opened it, allowing her to pass through first.

There were antechambers left and right around the base of a spiral stair. She followed his quick step up to a landing with more antechambers. They didn't pause, though he gestured to the left. "My rooms. My guards and valet are usually here, but they have leave to enjoy Beltane. Across are the rooms Androw's sons share when they are here. The eldest is away with Androw. His other son is fostered. His daughter is married."

Were they only *his* children? Lady Kirstine had nine months of her own blood in them, at the very least. If even her own blood wasn't hers, did anything in this castle belong to her?

They reached the top of the stairs and surprised young Marial in the process of wrapping a heavy gray cloak around her shoulders.

She quickly curtsied as her gaze traveled between Skyra and Lachlann. "Lord, does my lady need me?"

"No, Marial. You may go down to the fires if you wish. Skyra here may be taking up residence, but that is for my sister to say."

"Oh, I see." Marial blinked, then repeated with complete understanding, "Yes, yes, I see. It will be safer."

"Have your worried for your safety?" He seemed genuinely concerned.

"Only sometimes, my lord, when there are new guests in the floors below or your guards are absent."

"Exactly so. Off with you. The fires are bright." To Skyra he said, "Lord Androw's rooms are through those doors."

She eyed the wide, heavy double doors and guessed there was a large antechamber where men could wait to speak with the lord away from the eyes of the castle folk. That meant the small, single door was Kirstine's. Marial had left the door ajar, and he pushed it open. "I don't know what arrangements can be made, but if you were here in some way—"

"I would be between her and anyone foolish enough to approach without permission." The antechamber was small and young Marial had use of most of it. A wide wardrobe stood in one corner. The bed was narrow, and a worktable was strewn with garments being sewn and mended. A basket of half-carded wool sat under a delicate spinning wheel. "If the lady agrees, I will take up her protection."

He cocked his head — she was beginning to recognize it as a sign that he was choosing his words. "And all that it entails?"

"To my ending," she answered. The words, like her name, came to her as ones she had said before. It was very clear to her now — to this lady she would pledge all. To Kirstine.

His judgment of her was still precarious, but he finally nodded. "We will see what she says of this plan. Before we leave, your ear."

"What would you have me know?"

"Should Androw not return, there are those at court who are ambitious, and I have care for my nephews as his heirs. Likewise, should something happen to Kirstine while he is gone, I fear there will be blood. Mostly theirs, of course."

"Of course. Though if she comes to harm that would mean I was dead. I intend to live a long life."

She was pleased to see him show his genuine amusement. "Brightly said. I shall expect no less."

"Is Lady Kirstine aware of these ambitions?"

"She's not a fool, and we have spoken of it."

"No, she is not a fool." Kirstine was intelligent and aware of the risks and contradictions in the world, and yet still capable of joy. Skyra heard again in her mind the sound of Kirstine's laughter rising in the night and nearly smiled at recalling the unabashed pleasure she'd shown in devouring her Beltane bread.

Her errant imagination suggested other hungers and Kirstine's possible pleasure. She tried — and failed — to banish the thought of Kirstine's kisses from her mind.

She turned to the stair, but Lachlann seized her arm and did not let go when she pulled. She resisted the urge to reach for her dagger. Had he sensed the depth and nature of her feelings?

His voice grated in his throat. "Tell me true."

She could only nod.

"You would take up her protection?"

Relieved that he had noticed nothing untoward in her manner, she lifted her chin and met his gaze without equivocation. They were equals in devotion to the preservation of what they loved. And this was love, she recognized. Her entire being tightened around this certainty. Love, and deeper at every thought of Kirstine, every minute near her, and at every mention of her name. "To my ending. I swear it."

He let her go. "I will see to your ending should it be otherwise."

"I understand." She said it seriously and meant it. But could not help but add, "Well, you could try."

It was good fortune that he laughed.

Chapter Fifteen

"So you decided all of this between the two of you? Am I to be consulted?"

Kirstine's heart was pounding, and it would have been a lie to blame the speed with which she'd climbed all three flights of stairs. The moment Skyra had left with Lachie she'd been consumed with curiosity. Something untamed and unbidden sent her after them as soon as she could excuse herself.

She put all the affront she could manage into her question, which was hard because she wanted to shout *yes* and *yes* again to their proposal. Her reaction was as irrational as it was imperative. No one could know.

She will know.

It was not a time to debate anything within herself. She summoned a frown as Lachie spluttered, "Of course you must agree, but there is no reason for you to object."

Skyra said nothing as she stood just behind Lachie's shoulder. Her gaze was shuttered, as if she were merely a soldier awaiting orders, but Kirstine saw the tension in her jaw and the too-casual way she tucked her hands in her belt.

She will know.

"You can work out the details as you wish, but my desire is that whenever *you* are here, *she* is here. Else your door is bolted. If you go abroad in a crowd or out riding, she will be with you."

Skyra gave a nod of agreement.

"There is no room," Kirstine protested. She should rage against anyone taking away the blissful hours she now had to herself each night. It would be a loss, this was true, but even so, the idea that she would mayhap play her harp for this woman and talk as two minds filled her with joyous anticipation.

Lachie shrugged. "Your rooms have held two more ladies sleeping in your sitting room, along with two maids in the antechamber, haven't they?"

"Not for quite some time." *And never again, save Skyra.* "That was for my last lying-in."

Lachie ignored her and spoke to Skyra. "I've a bed in my rooms that is long enough, though narrow."

Skyra nodded thanks.

Kirstine put her hands on her hips. It seemed best for Lachie to think her consent was grudging, though she was not sure why she thought so. "Can you at least read?"

Skyra nodded yet again.

"Have you gone mute?"

Skyra shook her head.

Kirstine allowed herself to show anger, but inside there was only laughter. "What have you read?"

Skyra's lips twitched as if she realized she now had to speak. "I've read..." The hint of merriment faded, and her fine, dark brows came together as she concentrated. "I've read... The labels on Breda's bottles, I read those easily. She asked me to write out instructions for a villager's headaches, and I could, passably. It didn't come easily, but I knew how."

It gave her a pang behind her heart to see Skyra struggle to recall something so simple as the name of a book. "I'm sorry, I didn't mean to cause distress."

"Do not be. I nearly— I remember the feel of vellum under my fingertips, but I can't see the words. So far, the only memories that have come back have been when I spoke without thinking."

Lachie spread his hands. "Are we settled now?"

"I suppose so." She attempted to pout and didn't look at Skyra.

::*She will know.*::

Know what? she asked herself crossly.

::*That you feel.*::

Feel what?

That peculiar warmth that spread like liquid fire when she imagined how Skyra's hair might feel in her hands — it melted her now.

Quiet, her voice husky, Skyra asked, "Are you all right?"

She mingled a lie with truth. "I'm tired. The day has been full and is not over."

"Can you rest?"

"The noblewomen who weren't here early enough wish to pass between the fires, and I will go with them. I like the drumming. I ran up to change into my heavy boots." Truth mingled with another lie — she had to hide the truth.

::*She will know anyway.*::

"I'll go with you, then."

Lachie turned to the stairs with a laugh. "See? All settled? That wasn't difficult."

"Lachlann," Kirstine called after him. "What about boots? Might you spare a pair?" She gestured toward where she was almost certain she could see hose poking through at Skyra's toes.

Skyra made to protest, but Kirstine forestalled her with, "Don't be a fool. Even his old boots are excellent."

Lachie paused one step down the stairs, clearly unamused. "My valet has gone out to the bonfires."

She favored him with a sunny smile. "Is it safe for my bodyguard to have wet feet?"

His sigh was loud. "I'll return with a pair."

"And what about the bed?"

"That's going to have to wait until tomorrow."

"I can sleep anywhere. A chair would be fine," Skyra interjected.

"No, it wouldn't." Kirstine attempted to sound commanding and knew she had failed utterly.

Skyra's pale eyes held patient reassurance. "For one night I can manage."

Lachie spread his hands in acceptance. "She can manage. I'll fetch the boots, though they'll be too big."

"Some wool tufts in the toe and it'll be fine. Thank you, dearest of brothers."

It was easier to fuss at Lachie than it was to contemplate the next moment, when she would be alone with Skyra. She had no word for the sensation that ran through her. It was a shimmer like sunlight on a fast-running river, rippling behind her heart and down through her hips, into her knees, and now she felt it in her fingertips.

::*She will know.*::

Kirstine fixed a briskly efficient smile on her face and led Skyra deeper within her rooms. "In midsummer, when the wind turns seaward, it can be stifling hot in these rooms. I have a pallet I use to sleep on the balcony — the Lady's Watch. It will be better than the floor tonight."

"I will be fine."

Of that Kirstine had no doubt. Gaze always averted, she gave Skyra a brief tour ending on the Lady's Watch, near breathless all the while. A rising wind snapped at her cloak, but it was worth the cold to point out the bonfire and hear the voices in the bailey joined in song and laughter. The shrill swirl of a fiddle rose from the direction of the kitchens.

"When the drumming reaches its peak in the night, you can feel it in the stones. If it is early enough when we return, I'll play my harp to join their magic," she concluded.

"It's lovely out here." Skyra looked down at the stone tiles. "Beautiful."

"Isn't it though? I am here most summer nights." She thrust her hands into her pockets to quell the desire to touch Skyra's arm or her hair, her face. *What is wrong with me?*

::This is as it should be.::

The voice that continued to speak in her head didn't bring her any comfort. Was she ill? Was she dreaming? Something momentous was rising along with the drums of Beltane.

Skyra's face was turned away, but Kirstine still heard her low question. "Is this arrangement acceptable to you? That I should be always near?"

Kirstine tightened her jaw to hold back inexplicable words of welcome, of promise. She realized the coin in her pocket was hot against her clenched hand.

::Courage now. She already knows.::

Skyra turned away from the curling flames of the bonfires, from the music and clamor. The light from the inner chamber was enough to catch the fear in the pale eyes and to show the will it took for Skyra to hold her gaze.

She's afraid? Of me?

::She already knows.::

If she spoke a word, she would speak too many.

::There are never too many between your heart and hers.::

"Yes." The word vibrated between them like a plucked string. "It is acceptable."

Too much. She had shown too much. The fear she saw in Skyra's eyes vanished and something else was there, a look she had never seen in another before.

Skyra said only, with the softness of a songbird's gliding wings, "Oh my love."

Kirstine put her hands to her face — not to stop those words from reaching her, but to pull them to her. To never be able to deny that they had pierced her and found a fire inside her that matched.

Skyra made a small sound, ardent and pained, but Lachlann's steps were suddenly loud in the other room.

"We're out here, Lachie. Join us." How could her voice sound so natural? Inside her skin the world had been turned over and was still turning over, and she knew the only way to stop it was to take hold of Skyra and never let go.

"Boots." He plunked them on a small table near the door.

Boots.

If Kirstine drew more than the shallowest of breaths she would collapse in hysterics. Boots, as if they could possibly matter.

Boots.

Chapter Sixteen

What have I done?

Every part of Skyra's body could measure the distance between her and Kirstine. Scarcely more than arm's reach, but with her brother suddenly there, they seemed now on opposites sides of a fast-running river with no bridge between them.

What have I done?

Showed your courage, a thin voice of gold whispered in her mind.

Courage? No, it was madness, sheer madness to have let those words, three short words, find the air. *Oh my love,* she had said, and it felt like an echo of a past not hers and a harbinger of her own future. She had wandered far, and a very great way from all her memories, and all of it had led her here, to this truth.

Oh my love.

Faintly, an echo. ::*Oh my love.*::

She had meant to remark on the light from the bonfires and the moon. Had meant to be silent and watchful. To speak little — oh, and hadn't she spoken only a little?

Three words with the entire heavens and earth in them?

What sense she had of her past told her that she didn't lack for courage, and that her courage was not rooted in recklessness. To have spoken so to Kirstine *was* reckless, and now Kirstine's face was closed, her eyes in shadow.

"Do you think they will suit you, Skyra?"

"Yes." To Lachlann she tried to sound less tense. "I thank you sincerely."

How could they be discussing boots, of all things?

Again, that thread of golden voice spoke in her head. ::*Her eyes are the truth.*::

They are too dark to see.

::*Never.*::

"There is a cluster of ladies and their retinue gathered on the ground floor. Waiting for you, I gathered?"

"Would you tell them I'll be right down?" Kirstine's voice was free of tension or haste.

"Of course." He looked back and forth between them. "This arrangement will work?"

"Yes," Kirstine said firmly.

"I'll have the bed brought up tomorrow. You'll dine at my table, and I'll arrange for Captain Egann to add you to the clanguard allotment."

"That will be appreciated," Skyra answered, equally firm.

He gave a pleased nod and took his leave.

"I should put these on." Skyra gestured at the boots once Lachlann's footsteps had grown distant.

Kirstine moved a little closer, and her face came into the light from the moon. "Tell me I did not mishear you."

"The boots—"

"Do you deny the words?"

Her voice grated, not because the words were unwilling, but because they burst out of her. "Not to you, never. I will *never* deny you."

"Skyra..."

Her name in that beautiful voice gave her the strength to meet Kirstine's gaze again. Her eyes were deep wells of silken dark, and in the depths there was a light that shone only for Skyra to see. To somehow trust.

She went to her knees. "My lady."

"Not that," Kirstine whispered. "We are alone."

"My love," she breathed out. For all her armor and weapons she felt as fragile as a newborn chick.

Kirstine's face was full of wonder and confusion as she gazed down at Skyra. "What is happening?"

"I don't know. Except that it is truth. Fate, if Fate cared."

"I don't—" Kirstine turned her head sharply at the sound of footsteps approaching. "Boots."

"Boots," Skyra echoed. She stumbled to her feet and seized the pair Lachlann had brought.

"Lady Kirstine?" A woman's voice, tinged with impatience, called from the inner chamber. "Where are you?"

"Here," Kirstine said, leaving the Lady's Watch to join the newcomer. "With my new bodyguard."

Their voices fell into conversation and Skyra quickly sat in one of the oaken chairs and stripped off her tattered boots in favor of the new ones. Of quality leather and well oiled, they were too long in toe, but the heel was a good fit. The soles had been mended recently, but it was an excellent job. Even new, her old boots had not been this serviceable.

The light was low, but she laced them as best she could around her calves, tucked her trousers into the tops, and stepped into the inner chamber.

The newcomer was one of the court ladies some years younger than Kirstine, with curls of dark hair escaping from her hood.

Skyra thought to bow, slightly, then took up a position as a silent shadow. Let the court believe she was a statue and not see that she was utterly lost in heart and mind and body to their lady.

Kirstine had elicited the other woman's help with changing into her own boots and was ready, her manner that of a lighthearted woman ready for a night walk to the bonfires. Skyra could only hope that her demeanor was as effective as Kirstine's at hiding the magnitude of what had passed between them on the balcony.

She might even have thought it never happened, until Kirstine turned to her, and her eyes held that light, so deep. "Shall we?"

"Yes, my lady."

"Yes," Kirstine said, and once again, "Yes."

Yes.

She needed nothing more.

Chapter Seventeen

They reached the bottom of the spiral stairs to find a crowd of ten women and children. Skyra spied the sack she'd carried from Breda's only that morning. It felt a lifetime ago.

It was no moment to ask if she could claim her shield and helm — Kirstine was already in the great hall beyond. She moved briskly as she drew on gloves and chattered with the younger girls about importance of Beltane cleansing as the seasons turned to new planting and brighter skies.

As Skyra fell into step with the intent to catch up to Kirstine, she met the startled gazes of several court ladies. She acknowledged them with a nod but said nothing.

The auspices of Beltane are always good, Breda had said. Mayhap they were something else as well, something that birthed a wild desire inside her and had drawn reckless words, three short words, to her lips.

The drums grew louder with every step closer to the Beltane field. The fires were much larger now, and clusters of townsfolk were dancing in groups around them.

The rising wind carried smoke, shouts and laughter, verses of song and, sparkling tunes from multiple pipers. There was only a thin line of blue at the horizon, then even that was gone, and night was fully upon them.

She hastened her pace when she saw several white-robed figures along the road. It was the local priest, she saw, with attendants. He carried a heavy wooden cross on his rigid shoulder and called out at random, "Repent of this pagan sacrilege!"

No one was paying him much mind until Kirstine and her group of ladies caught his attention. He made as if to block her way. "Lady, this is sacrilege! Pagan idolatry that risks your soul. You should set an example for your people!"

"That's what I'm doing," Kirstine blithely answered, her voice raised to be heard over the drums. "You are welcome to join in. The old gods won't mind, and you may get to know *my* people better."

One gloved hand brushed the air, and he stepped aside, but not without bluster. Lady Kirstine was obeyed, but Skyra did not like the fever in the man's eyes.

"Let him keep his kirk, and I'll keep Beltane," she heard Kirstine say to a lady next to her as they entered the field.

"I shall have both," the lady responded. "Beltane tonight and penance tomorrow."

"That sounds exhausting."

"If I don't go tomorrow, I could not be here tonight. My husband listens more and more to the priest, who says his law is higher than any mortal lord's."

Their conversation was lost as Skyra fell into the memory of the tea-driven dream, of a boat of light sailing to ruin against a dark wind.

::She is the light.::

And what is the dark wind?

::Darkness always comes to extinguish the light.::

She shook her head to free her mind of the insidious voice. Exhaustion and overwrought feelings, that was the truth of it.

The drums were deafening when they finally came abreast of the players. They faced each other in a broad circle, and Skyra saw that most of the drums were made of hollowed tree trunks stretched over with thick, tough skins and struck with mallets in both hands of the player.

Other folk struck hammers on overturned iron pots. Some of the dancers held smooth river rock in their hands, clacking them together in the same rhythm as the drums. Still more shook and pounded tambourines.

It was raucous and untamed. Everything, she was certain, that an hour's penance in the kirk was not.

When she looked again at Kirstine she found the dark gaze on her face. The flames seemed to dance in her eyes, and it matched the twining, shivering heat that rose in Skyra's body.

Kirstine said something but it was lost in the drums.

Her mind heard the words anyway.

::*Let us walk through together*.::

Madness or magic, did it matter? Their steps fell into the rhythm of the drums, slow and steady. The orange-red flames were tall and bright, with yellow sparks leaping even higher into the night sky. As they reached the point equally between the two bonfires, the heat was more intense than the noonday sun.

Even so, it was no match for her own fires. Whatever words had been said, Kirstine could not, should not, have any idea of Skyra's wild imaginings of kisses and skin, of secret music.

Better it burn me than her.

Kirstine paused to look up at her, her head cocked in speculation. She leaned toward Skyra as if she would speak over the drums, forcing Skyra to bring her ear near to Kirstine's lips.

"Let it burn us both, then."

Skyra's breath left her as if she'd been struck a heavy blow, and she was all at once aware of how many pairs of eyes would be watching their every gesture. She managed to answer, "You don't know this fire."

"Not until today."

How to balance her desire and the pledge she had made only an hour ago? "I have promised to protect you."

"Are you dangerous?" Kirstine turned her head away as if she did not want to hear the answer.

What answer could she possibly make with anything like honesty? She would never harm Kirstine, but her mind filled with images of them together, with the ripe readiness of their bodies witnessed only by the moon and stars. Mayhap she came from a place where such knowledge between women was not forbidden, but here? Where Kirstine's children didn't even belong to her? Where, on the day when Kirstine opened the rites of Beltane for her people, an unkempt priest fearlessly shouted at her as if he had the power to be her judge?

She is married, Skyra reminded herself. Married, and not for you.

::*She has never been given a choice.*::

"I think." Her voice broke and she had to begin again, louder. "I think we stand in a dangerous moment."

Kirstine gave the slightest of nods. "I feel it. The danger." She stepped back to find and hold Skyra's gaze with eyes of midnight and silver stars. "And the magic. A magic no one else will understand."

"I don't know that I understand it."

Kirstine opened her cloak to draw something from her pocket. On her palm was a rune stone — not a stone, Skyra corrected herself. A coin that caught the fire's shifting light. On its face were the busts of two women in profile, their gazes locked on one another.

"Marial must have polished it." Kirstine sounded bemused. "I could have sworn this morning that it was still tarnished. Where did she find the time?"

"What is it?"

::*I was made on a night such as this, in a fire of molten gold. Made by Aphaea Artemis, made for the Beloved.*::

The words came into her mind so vividly, with boundless pride and bottomless sorrow, that the tender place on the side of her head pulsed with sudden pain.

Kirstine looked up at her, uncertainty in her eyes. "Did you hear—" She broke off and shook her head as if dizzied.

Skyra saw again the boat of light sailing to ruin against a dark wind. "Where did you get this thing?"

"A gift, brought to me by a young woman who was long ago a babe I helped birth. I was able to save both child and mother. It was the mother that found it."

This was beyond Skyra's ken. A gift of this coin in return for the gift of life — could such a thing be evil?

::*I am not a gift. I am not evil.*::

"Then what are you?"

The question was spoken by both of them.

Kirstine put her other hand to her throat.

A warning chill ran down Skyra's spine. She covered the coin with her hand, trapping it between their palms. "Put it away."

::*After long years in the sea, I have a purpose.*::

"Put it away," Skyra repeated.

With a mute nod, Kirstine returned the coin to her pocket.

Skyra let her hand fall to her side and bowed slightly, servant to mistress, and hoped that no one had observed any strangeness in them for these past few minutes.

Kirstine resumed her path between the fires, and they reached the cool darkness beyond them. The drums had increased their pace once again. A long chain of men and women snaked around the base of one fire, then circled the other, and back again. The high tin clamor of the tambourines and pipes could have woken any sleeping gods, Skyra thought, for they were surely giving her a headache. Any sense of the song itself was lost in the continual thump and boom of the drums.

The side of her head was now throbbing in that same rhythm. She felt as if a memory was very close, a memory as red as the heart of the bonfires, and it was too much. There was already too much fire.

::*There will always be too much fire now.*::

Another of the court ladies, sharp of nose and shoulders, was asking Kirstine about her own husband's flocks and a grazing meadow.

"Tomorrow, Lady Liosa. I'm afraid the smoke and drums have given me a headache."

They were some distance from the bonfires now. The lack of light made Skyra caution, "We are mayhap too far from the crowd."

"Indeed. I would like to go to my rooms now." Kirstine lightly touched the other woman's arm. "It has been a very long day."

"I understand," Lady Liosa answered, but Skyra saw falsity in the smile that accompanied the words. Her gaze flicked over Skyra with little interest.

Disappearing into her duties, she offered her arm. "My lady, may I lend you support? It is a long walk back."

"Thank you, yes."

Kirstine's gloved hand rested lightly on Skyra's forearm as they walked one last time between the bonfires.

The drums, the dancers, the flames. There was whispering in her head from behind the wall in her mind. Red memory, black night, silver stars, and always the flames.

Too much fire, Skyra thought.

::*There will always be too much fire.*::

Chapter Eighteen

Kirstine remembered little of their return to the castle. Her head was heavy with the smoke, and her ears were ringing from the noise. Beltane had never affected her this way, but all of this day was a series of nevers.

This woman next to her, leading the way because Kirstine did not care where they went as long as it was away from the din and together, this woman had spoken of love and looked at her in a way Kirstine didn't recognize. And this talisman, the coin, had spoken to them of fires and goddesses. Both of these things were impossible.

Another impossibility she added to the list — the yearning in her own heart for something unknown and unnamed, made in starlight and dancing like lightning along all of her skin and in deep and sweet places.

When women whispered of pleasures and delights, Kirstine had smiled as if she understood. Androw had once called her cold, so she allowed him to think he warmed her.

It was safer. It had protected the broken heart of the girl she'd once been, who'd believed the old songs of love and valor.

You are still married to him, she reminded herself. You promised obedience and fidelity, though he did not.

::*Is that love?*::

She pushed the voice away even as she answered to herself that no, it had not been about love. It had never been about love. It was a contract made without a single word of say from her.

All at once she realized where her thoughts were leading. Away from her past and her compulsory vows. Toward love, the music of it, the fire of it, the feel of it. The fever in her body, the pounding of her heart, the chill that tightened her skin — she could not think what she might do with Skyra, but it had no comparison to the obedient and required duties of her marital bed. Another aspect of the marriage contract she had had no say over.

She'd been delivered like cargo into a better-than-expected alliance and found her new husband and his people dismissive of all the qualities her mother had instilled into Kirstine: to show grace, share songs, honor life, and always have care for those not so fortunate in the circumstance of their birth.

She was proud of what she'd been able to change in this place. Proud of the fed elders and children who knew how to read and add numbers. As they passed through the castle gate she found herself at last at the core of the grief that had overwhelmed her that first night alone in her rooms.

Her grief was not about what she'd done with these twenty years, but what she'd not been allowed to do.

Wasn't the proof that there could be more walking next to her?

"I gave Marial leave to enjoy Beltane for as long as she wishes," she murmured, and she did not want to admit even to herself why she told Skyra that. "The Night Watch bell doesn't ring tonight."

Kirstine paused at the tower door to make sure the clanguards there knew who Skyra was, and then began the climb up the spiral stairs. Behind her she heard the clank of metal and glanced back to see Skyra gathering the sack she'd brought with her only that afternoon. Why did it feel as if every minute with Skyra was a lifetime together?

Her vision misted over to see two women in warm cloaks choosing their path at a crossroads. One carried a harp, the other an axe. They had so little, and they had everything, including their freedom.

She had fainted once, long ago, during her first confinement. The same gray rags fluttering in her eyes threatened her now. No, she thought, I will not swoon. It was her strength she wanted Skyra to know. The pulse along her neck went ever faster at the thought of being alone with Skyra and speaking anything she wished to her. To speak of love, somehow.

They met no one along the way to the top of the tower. She was glad to have thought to close the door from the Lady's Watch and that of her own chamber. Her rooms were blissfully warm.

Skyra followed her into the sitting room. Kirstine pointed out a corner where the bulky sack could be set down and out of the way. Its clank on the floor was followed by a swooshing whirl as Skyra pulled her axe from her back and set it, blade up, against the wall.

After slinging her cloak over her chair, followed by her gloves, Kirstine lit a rush from the fire and transferred the flame to the near lamps. By their steady light she returned to the door, wanting it closed and locked. The effort to close it, however, seemed too much for her dizzied head, and she steadied herself by resting her forehead on the cool, solid wood.

Then Skyra was there, behind her, lending her weight to pushing the heavy door closed. One of Skyra's braids tickled against her ear. She fumbled with the door's lock and managed to secure it, even as she felt the rise and fall of Skyra's chest against her back.

Again, she rested her forehead on the wood, reaching within herself for the strength to do what this moment required. To accept what she could not deny.

She heard Skyra swallow hard.

If you mean it, Kirstine told herself, whispers are not necessary. She drew what shaky breath she could to say clearly, "I spoke truth, earlier. About this fire."

She turned to put her back to the door and fixed her gaze on the place where Skyra's armor framed the smooth column of her throat.

"Kirstine." Skyra's voice grated with so much pain that Kirstine made herself look into the moonlight-on-ice eyes.

Oh, she thought. Not pain.

The future spilled open.

She brushed the long hair and braids from between them and brought her fingers to the tender skin of Skyra's lips. Skyra was trembling, this strong, powerful woman, and Kirstine knew it was because of her.

This fire matched her own, and all her long years of practiced reason fell away. Yesterday and tomorrow ceased to be and there was only now, Beltane night. Now.

"If there is to be fire," she murmured, "let it burn us both."

She raised her lips to find Skyra's, to kiss her and finally be united.

Chapter Nineteen

Skyra's arms were strong around her, lifting her to the very tips of her toes. Their lips parted and met again as Kirstine wrapped her arms around Skyra's neck. The air was filled with shivering intensity that beat at Kirstine's ears and eyes.

If there was a center to all things, it was this fated kiss, Kirstine thought. How had earth or heaven existed before it? How had she?

The pulse of Skyra's heart was against her mouth. She drew back only to gasp for air and this time when their lips met, they opened to each other. There was an exquisite moment of soft wonder at the brush of Skyra's tongue. All gone a heartbeat later as Skyra pulled the hood from Kirstine's head, freeing her unbound hair. Then Skyra's hands were in her hair, and she buried her face in it with a disbelieving moan.

Her fingers fumbled at the ties and rings of Skyra's breastplate. Though their bodies were as close as they had ever been, it was not close enough.

The sensation of swooning was upon her again as she realized that Skyra's hands were at the belt of her kirtle, loosening it. Urgency filled her for Skyra's touch in all her private places, though to what end she had no idea. She knew only it was necessary and wanted. It served the conspiring Fates that had brought them both to this moment.

Skyra's armor fell to the floor with a thud, and to Kirstine she seemed even taller. Her hands explored the broad shoulders and long neck before setting to work on unlacing the leather and cloth tightly bound to Skyra's chest.

"That can wait," Skyra said in her ear.

There was cool air all around her legs as her kirtle floated quietly down to join the armor. Kirstine shivered, not from the cold, but from the heat of Skyra's body against hers. She claimed Skyra's mouth again for another kiss that felt like a promise, but Kirstine had no idea what that promise might be.

Her chemise was open, and Skyra's chest was against her naked breasts. She pushed down her hose. She wouldn't think of what she knew of lovemaking. It was useless to her in Skyra's arms. In her mind was an empty realm, she could see it plainly now. It had waited, as she had all these years, to learn the unraveling magic wrought by the sliding brush of a single fingertip along the inside of her thigh.

She whimpered and felt the chill of Skyra pushing away from her.

"Have I hurt you?"

Kirstine marveled at the redness of Skyra's lips, the lines of tension in her face, the unbound passion in her eyes. "It isn't hurt. I am...undone."

Skyra looked down then and steadied herself with a hand on the door behind Kirstine. "I knew you would be beautiful. But I did not *know*."

Then her mouth was on Kirstine's breasts. They had, for all her life, existed to feed children and please in her marital bed. With the rasp of Skyra's teeth they suddenly felt as if they belonged to her for a reason, this reason, to send sharp crackles like lightning along her shoulders and stabbing down her stomach to strike fire in places no longer private, because Skyra had dropped to her knees and was kissing her there. Tasting her there.

Her legs supported her for a minute, no more, then she lost her grasp on the lock. There was no fear, however, because Skyra looked up at her, eyes hooded, lips wet, and helped her to slide easily to the floor. She was on her back, and only breathing was required of her as Skyra's long body stretched between her legs as she resumed pleasuring Kirstine with her mouth.

Her breath came in great gasps. I am undone, she thought again. There was lightning everywhere now, purple and sharp and hot, and tears, her tears, and the feel of Skyra's hair in her hands. Only that and Skyra's mouth on her remained real as rapture beyond heaven claimed her.

* * *

What have I done? Skyra asked herself this question again, but it was not with the despair of earlier in the day. Kirstine was in her arms, her body relaxing into the aftermath of abandon.

She would live a thousand lives for one moment such as this. Mayhap she had. "Oh my love," she whispered.

Kirstine's lips curved into a smile of such languor and ease that Skyra smiled too. "I didn't know," she murmured.

"Know what?" Skyra kissed the side of her mouth.

"This magic." Kirstine turned her head just enough to brush her lips against Skyra's. Her eyes widened and she tasted the depths of Skyra's mouth. "Is that... Is that how I taste?"

"Yes."

"It's sweet, and not."

"Yes."

Her face filled with curiosity, Kirstine put her hand down and touched herself — for the first time, Skyra realized, that was not about blood, childbirth, and cleanliness.

"All the gossip and giggles, of how many times, and hints about size. None of it, not one word of it, was about this silk."

With a rising pulse, Skyra watched Kirstine's fingers slip into the wet, full folds between her own legs. "It is a gift, don't you think?"

"Your mouth is a gift." Kirstine's voice had tightened, and Skyra tore her gaze from the dance of Kirstine's fingertips to see that her love's eyebrows had arched in growing pleasure. "Your mouth there, it was... I have no adequate words."

After lightly trailing her fingers down Kirstine's stomach she joined her touch to Kirstine's, showing her the magic she knew until Kirstine's breath caught. "There is this, too, that we may share."

Her lips captured one peak of Kirstine's breasts. Her tongue played with the taut nipple, drawing a shuddering coo from Kirstine. Her fingers sought lower between Kirstine's legs and circled there.

Kirstine lifted her hips in response, and Skyra followed the invitation to be inside and feel her.

Silk, Kirstine had called it. It was beyond that. The taste of Kirstine's wet was still in her mouth and in her mind were dim echoes of other women. Similar in the ways of a woman's body. Nothing like the wonder of Kirstine as she moved with a flowing urgency, eyes open and wide with disbelief and anticipation both.

She reached deeply inside Kirstine, savoring the muscles and soft flesh against her fingers. Her mind filled with the pleasure of these mysteries and the music of Kirstine's gasps.

Kirstine covered her own mouth with her hand when her cry of release escaped her. Even as she relaxed, Skyra filled her again and locked her gaze with Kirstine and took her once more. Kirstine cried out a second time, a frantic, "Yes," and again, "Yes."

And again, "Yes."

PART FOUR

Bringer of the Long Night

Chapter Twenty

The high narrow windows of her bedchamber held only early, gray morning light. Kirstine closed her eyes again. She was too warm to move and, anyway, Skyra's arm was over her hip and their ankles were crossed as Skyra nestled behind her.

"How long do we have?"

Skyra's quiet question startled her only slightly. "How did you know I was awake?"

"Your breathing changed."

"You've been listening to me breathe?"

Skyra kissed her gently between her shoulder blades. "Yes, and I shall do so whenever I may."

In all her life, Kirstine had never wondered what it would feel like to be completely opened, to let another see the true form of her heart. As a girl, her mother had cautioned that her inner thoughts might be the one thing that were hers and hers alone. Her body would, someday, belong to her husband. Her work and even her harp would exist to serve and give pleasure to others.

As a young woman trying to survive in a strange land with strange customs, she had never displayed the true feelings of her heart. No one need know that snow tasted like sugar on her tongue, and her husband's voice sounded like an untuned harp in her ears. That the laughter of children felt like sunshine, or that when she held a hot mug of tea in her hands and rested it against her chest she wondered if that was what it might feel like to be loved. To love.

She knew the answer to that now. If this were indeed love — and how would she know if it were?

::*You know.*::

I know.

Skyra's hand wandered from Kirstine's hip to her breast. In a more meaningful tone, she asked again, "How long do we have?"

The desire to yield to the sweet promise of Skyra's caresses was very strong. But the morning light was indeed cold, and she needed cool reason on this day, the first day of her own life.

She stilled Skyra's hand. "Mayhap not enough time for that."

Skyra withdrew her hand and separated their bodies. "I will never persist when you say it cannot be. In this — I've been thinking as you breathed—"

Kirstine laughed. "Tell me."

"Only here, when the door is locked, are we other than Lady Kirstine and her bodyguard."

She rolled over so there would be no misunderstanding between them. She couldn't help but smile at the sight of Skyra's hair. It was tousled and full of knots that Kirstine longed to brush out as they talked by the fire.

Skyra went on earnestly. "But even here, you are allowed to say what can be between us and when."

"As can you. Else you are a servant, and I do not wish to rule you."

"You do." The words were said with a smile, but the echo behind them was heavy with truth.

"You know what I mean. That's not what I want."

Though her hands stayed away, the look in Skyra's eyes caressed her face. "What do you want?"

"For there to be enough time." She forced herself to sit up, else the warmth of the bed would undo her resolve. "Marial will tap in a few minutes. I am usually awake this early." Through the bedchamber doorway she could see their scattered clothes and the story they told.

"I need to have slept somewhere other than your bed."

"Did you sleep?"

"For a time. You in my arms was all the dreaming I needed." Skyra had sat up as well and pulled the blankets around both their shoulders.

"Sweet words. They can only be spoken here."

"I know."

In a rush, because she didn't want give the world outside the door the power to break them, she said, "There will be times when I will seem distant. When I cannot smile at you, or ask your leave, or even allow you to speak. All of that will be for other eyes." She pulled Skyra's lips to hers for a warm kiss of promise. "When we are alone, when the door is locked, we will be two women, and all that we would like to be. Do you like the harp and song?"

"I do." Skyra's eyes flashed with affectionate anticipation. "I believe I will like it even more in future days."

"I hope so. I was going to play it last night, but..." There were foolish tears of happiness in her eyes now. "There was other music to be made."

"My love." Skyra brushed hair back from Kirstine's face. "Magic or Fate, it is my choice to live and love you, even if it proves fatal. I will not be parted from you."

::*Never parted.*::

"That coin," Kirstine said carefully. "Without its reassurance, I think I might be shocked and afraid. I cannot explain how I know I can trust it. Trust *this*."

Skyra's tone became philosophical. "There is no time to try to explain it right now. If there was enough time, then I'd rather it were spent in other pursuits."

"As would I." She kissed Skyra until their breath grew heated. All else might have followed but Marial's quiet tap on the door sent them stumbling to retrieve pillows from the floor and restore the blankets to something like order.

"She will check again in a few minutes." Kirstine pulled on her sleeping gown and picked up yesterday's clothes, folding them as she normally would have. The coin she pulled from her kirtle pocket to set on the mantel. Its face was once again begrimed, showing neither of the women that had shone in the lights of the Beltane fires.

Whatever it was, it could wait.

A distinct sense of vexation blossomed in her mind. ::*I like that not.*::

She frowned at it. "None of that or I will put you in a drawer."

"Here." Skyra was holding out a mug filled with water. "I am parched."

She drank thirstily before saying, "I wonder why."

Skyra's color rose, much to Kirstine's delight. Even so, her voice was exceedingly smug. "I regret nothing. I believe you don't either."

Kirstine closed her eyes as her mind filled with her exploration of Skyra's body after they'd had the sense to move to the warm bed. Her long, firm muscles were things of wonder. As were the soft swells of her small breasts. Most wonderful was the tangle of hair that grew damp from Kirstine's teasing, and then was soaked as Kirstine tasted, finally, the essence of her. The sweetness of it had been on her lips and smeared across her cheeks.

She opened her eyes with a sudden realization. "We need to wash our faces."

Laughter bubbled up from Skyra's chest. "Good thing there is water and cloth. Let me get dressed."

Skyra bending over for her trousers was the undoing of all Kirstine's intentions. Sprays of freckles decorated her shoulders, and there were scars on her back and legs, likely from slashes of swords. Kirstine wanted to learn them all.

Now she saw only the curve of Skyra's body and its invitation to delight.

From close behind her she said, "There is time for this, for I think you are near ready," and she put her hands on Skyra's hips.

Skyra made no pretense as she fumbled her way to Kirstine's chair. "Please."

"Quickly." Last night, at her first taste of Skyra, she had felt drunk with desire. The feeling came back now as she could see Skyra's unfolding beauty. "You are not alone in need."

She slid to her knees and, all in a rush, pulled Skyra's legs to her shoulders so she could taste and love her completely. This was a new thirst, and she wanted to learn better what made Skyra groan. In future days and nights there would be more time, but for now, this was enough.

Skyra made that sound she had made last night. Kirstine's hair drifted over her stomach and legs, and she made that sound again.

"Oh, beautiful," Kirstine whispered to her. "Oh my love, how beautiful."

Chapter Twenty-One

"You have been out and about the countryside so much these past months." Lachie quieted his gray as they conversed in the stable door, he on his way in and she on her way out. "It agrees with you."

"Midsummer will find me happier than I have been in a while."

He scoffed and kept his voice low. "I don't miss Androw either. There is more discipline in the rank."

It was true that Androw's absence was part of her happiness, and she would let him think that was the entirety of it. "I thank you for finding me the means. I wasn't sure at first." She'd had no idea where time spent with Skyra would lead, had she? "It has worked out."

Lachie's gray sidled away from Kirstine's mare, and he quieted it again. "Where are you off to today?"

"We're off to the port, to consult the Port Master's maps. I should have thought of it earlier. Mayhap the names will stir Skyra's memory."

At this, Skyra nodded. Her silence was now well-known at court, and Kirstine was certain that only she knew how to read it. At the moment, Skyra was patiently waiting for an end to the conversation.

"A good thought." He looked inquiringly at Skyra.

"It may unlock something. I had hoped by now that I would recall more."

Skyra was well healed in body, and it showed in the glow of her hair and skin. But there was something in Skyra's past that Kirstine knew had to be a wound in her mind that good food and sleep didn't reach. She sometimes cried out in nightmare and once had murmured, "For this?"

"Will I see you at the practice ring when you return?"

"You will," Skyra said simply.

He grinned. "I've two lads asking to practice with axes."

"Good. In battle an axe wreaks chaos on those who trained only against swords and spears."

Kirstine saw Skyra frown as she spoke and had learned it meant that a memory was teasing at the edges of her mind, risking a headache. The wind off the sea would help. "Brother, you are blocking the stable door."

"Childish, Sister, when it was you who stopped me."

Skyra was openly smiling as their horses fell into a trot. The big bay she rode was no longer battle prime, but it had nuzzled at Skyra's hair at the moment they met, and it had been love at first sight.

The summer day was bright and breezy, and the road to the port was thick with carts and travelers.

"I would like to retire early tonight," she told Skyra.

Skyra, with studied nonchalance, answered, "As you like."

"Not for that — very well, yes for that. But I've not played my harp enough and there is a song I would sing you I've sung for no other."

In the silence she could feel Skyra holding back laughter.

"Another song," she muttered.

"You sing sweetly, my lady."

She looked the truth back at Skyra. *As do you.*

Skyra lowered her lashes in silent acknowledgment.

Sweet music. Her body would never have its fill of it. For everyone on the other side of Kirstine's door, Marial included, nothing had changed. She still lingered on the Lady's Watch, time to time, and played her harp, time to time. She sat in court and gave her judgments. She visited landholders and the miller for reports on grain yields and when it might come to be ground into meal. That she had resumed her habit of riding pleased everyone, it seemed.

She was most worried about Lachie, but even he seemed to discern nothing unusual between her and Skyra. He was glad she'd come to him for further training in her own defense and resharpened her skill at throwing her dagger. He didn't need to know that her real goal was to watch Skyra at practice.

She hadn't understood until she'd seen the axe in full arc overhead as Skyra herself spun on her toes — she'd had no idea the deadly beauty and sheer speed of it. Even Lachie watched now with nothing but admiration. The practice was bloodless, but she could imagine the river of red it created.

It was blood that troubled Skyra's mind — red memory she called it, the memory that would not come and stoppered all the rest of her life behind it.

It would come someday, Kirstine thought. It needn't be today. The summer green hills had never seemed so rich with flowers before, nor the sheep's wool so white and fine. The sky overhead was the color of Skyra's eyes in candlelight, bringing the warmth of summer into their life together.

I am blessed.

::You are, and she is.::

Have you a story to tell me today?

::No. I am unsettled and bored with stories.::

How can I help you with that?

::You cannot. I am lost.::

She still did not know what the coin was, exactly. It spoke to her mind, and to Skyra's. At first whispers, then shouts. It sometimes knew when someone was coming to their door. It was made by a goddess, it said, and that did not seem far-fetched to Kirstine. Didn't the kirk have its bits of bones and holy relics purported to heal and give solace?

The coin's voice in their minds, however, was wrapped in a sadness that Kirstine wished she could ease. Its melancholy sometimes lasted a week and it had yet to answer any of her many questions about its past and why it had come to her. I am lost, it would say, and leave her in silence.

The road widened and they were able to pass many of the carts. Her hood persisted in blowing off her head and she finally gave up pinning it back in place.

"You look more like you without it," Skyra offered.

"I think so too. The kirk can't make up its mind if we women should wear it morning, noon, or night, and then a ship arrives from Gaul full of new fashion. I would rather hear a new bard than discuss once more all the names for shades of red."

"I wonder what arrives today."

"Not new hoods with more wires and pins, I hope. I've noticed no one tells you to wear one."

"At least not twice," Skyra answered. "That includes that querulous priest. I don't like how bold he is. More every day, like the bullies who lurked in the woods near Breda's."

Skyra didn't say aloud that these priests could come with fire and weapons, but Kirstine knew the thought was in her mind. She didn't like the growing boldness of the kirk either, but her authority was not so absolute she could take on its rising power over daily life. At court only last week, one of the highborn lords had wanted to send for the priest to ask his opinion on a matter of law. She had been able to put it off, but the very idea chilled her. What would Androw have done at such a suggestion?

Just as water was wet, she knew that no one would have made such a suggestion to him.

There were vivid whitecaps showing on the distant waves, and the wind sharpened as they passed the gap in the long bluffs that served to guard the town from unwanted incursions from the port.

"There is a ship coming in," Skyra noticed. "Do you know its flag?"

"It looks like a merchant returning from Solring. The Port Master will know."

After the jarring from the ruts of the road, the solid wooden pier was welcome. Heads ducked and hats were doffed as she passed, and Kirstine was aware of many eyes turned toward Skyra as well.

Watchful eyes had clearly reported her arrival, and the Port Master greeted her before she had even dismounted. "Lady, what brings you to us today?"

Skyra was already off her bay and had come around to tie Kirstine's mare as was her habit. Kirstine swung her leg behind her to dismount and too late felt the toe of her boot catch the hem of the kirtle flounce Marial had added last month to keep the new fashion come from the Norse court. She teetered a moment trying to free her foot, her mare shied under her as if to help her balance, and then she fell.

Of course Skyra caught her.

::Of course.::

Skyra quickly set her on her feet, but her hands remained on Kirstine's arms. "Are you all right?"

She was embarrassed to look so foolish. "Yes, and I thank you. It's these stupid skirts. Fashion added that extra layer and it mocks me every day."

The Port Master was aghast. "Lady, you should have reined in next to the step."

"I know how to get off a horse," she snapped. "You're welcome to try it yourself in these skirts."

"Wouldn't that be a sight?"

She and Skyra did not join him in laughter.

Sobering, he asked again, "How may I be of aid to you?"

"We would like to look at your maps of seas and lands to the north, the most detailed you have."

"Come away in, then."

The Port Master's office was busy with clarks at several tables making lists of goods changing hands. Bolts of fabric rested along the wall, and some of them were of that ugly red mixed with brown that had court ladies in a tizzy. There was a particularly heated discussion between a clark gesticulating at a ledger and a weathered, dark-of-face captain who swayed as if he still stood upon his ship. The air was pungent with the crowd of bodies and the pervasive smell of fish and onion.

The Port Master gave her his own table to use and went to the sheaths of vellum that hung over a series of dowels anchored high on the wall. He chose three, sliding them off one by one onto his arm to keep them unwrinkled. Once they were spread on the table, he left them to it.

Kirstine didn't know what she expected to happen now. Skyra bent close, her lips moving as she silently tasted the names of ports marked with sails and castles marked with crosses.

"Can you make sense of them, or can I help?"

"We are here." Skyra put her finger on the cross next to the word "Drummbhaile." Moving her finger north she stopped on a long curve of narrow land. "This is the island we could see from the top of the hill as we rode in."

"Yes."

With her hand waving to take in the rest of the map, she added, "And this is the north, near and far."

"Breda thought you were from very far."

Skyra bent close again, peering at the top of the map where land ended. "Vogan? Skalhold? Nidaros? These mean nothing to me."

Gently, Kirstine suggested, "There is no hurry. If it is all new to you, then it is new. A lesson. I will ask for a map to the south and refresh my own memory of the names from home. Take your time. I'm not bored."

Skyra nodded absently, her gaze intent on the map though she shook her head.

The Port Master was happy to bring Kirstine a map of Galrandel's shores. The din of the many conversations faded to nothing, and she visited her home again in her mind. She doubted she would ever see it, and if she did it would no longer be home.

An hour later, mayhap a bit more, Skyra sighed. "Nothing. Though my eyes go back to Skalhold, I think it is because its name was said to me as a place I should go, not that I was there. It is here, to the north and west."

Kirstine set aside her map to look. "On Island? We receive ships from there, though the sailors say it is not all ice, and they speak of steam and boiling water bubbling from the ground."

"That I think I would remember."

"Well, we now know that Breda was likely right. You are from the far North. The very far North— What is that?"

She realized that there had been shouting on the pier and more voices had joined it.

"Another ship sighted, at the horizon," Skyra said.

The Port Master hurried outside, his sighting glass in hand. With nothing more to be gleaned from the maps, they followed him onto the increasingly crowded pier. He had clambered up a ladder to a small lookout.

"What do you see?" Kirstine called up to him.

"It's one of ours," the Port Master reported. "A merchant karfi. I think it's the *Drystyk Hauk*."

"More goods, then?"

"It was bound for Stavanger, on the mainland. It was not due back so soon. Lady, it flies a black banner."

The warm summer wind turned to ice on Kirstine's skin.

Chapter Twenty-Two

Kirstine had gone pale, and a knell of alarm filled Skyra's mind. "What does that mean?"

"Ill news. Returning from its next port with ill news. A death, likely." Kirstine's hands began to shake.

Nearby a man bolted away on a horse to carry the news of a black banner ship coming into port.

"A king?"

"We will know before nightfall."

Her husband, Skyra thought. That's who she believes it will be, and she will not say it aloud.

Even in their private time, Kirstine had said little about her husband, but enough for Skyra to understand she need never be jealous of him. He'd never held Kirstine's heart or genuine respect, and she knew she had both.

It might not be him, she reasoned, and she should live each day with wonder and joy because he might yet return. Just as her memory was behind a dark wall, the contemplation of a future without Kirstine was also behind a wall, this one of her own choosing.

"Let us find a place to wait, where you can get some ale and food." She'd seen a stable and inn not far back up the road. "Come. We'll walk and lead the horses."

Kirstine was not alone in her fears. It was clear in the way some folk abruptly stopped talking and made way for her that they, too, thought the news might be about her husband. Or, her son, Skyra thought.

The stableman took their horses and the innkeeper's wife took charge of Kirstine in a matronly way, ushering them past curious eyes into her own sitting room. A short time later she brought a pot of steeping tea and wedges of mutton pie.

Some of Kirstine's color came back after sips of tea and several small bites of food.

"Do you think wishing you might never see someone again is the same as wishing ill on them?" Her tone was philosophical, but Skyra wasn't fooled.

"No, I don't. If this is the worst news, you cannot blame yourself."

"I didn't truly try to stop him."

"Would you have been successful?"

"No."

She cast about for ways to help pass the long waiting time for the ship to come in with the tide. "Did you bring the coin?"

Kirstine wordlessly drew it from her pocket and handed it to Skyra. "It's having a sad day."

She had not held it much, and though at times she thought it had whispered to her heart, she'd usually heard its voice clearly only when they both held it. It was a magical thing, and not for the likes of her to understand. The folk of the kirk, while deep in tales of water made into wine, would no doubt think it the work of their devil.

::I am no devil's work.::

Then what are you?

::I was made by Aphaea Artemis—::

I know all that. Forged in fire, yes, and given some magic by the goddess. But what are you for?

::I don't know! I am lost. I am lost—::

Kirstine put her hand on Skyra's. "What's going on?"

::—into the sea, where I drifted on Poseidon's waves. I was meant for the Beloved to hold, to give the grace of the sacred Artemis to her.::

You've been in the sea all these years?

::No. There was the sea and a fish, and a larger fish, and a boat, and a pocket, and I was not touched by woman until the old one found me and kept me as a gift for the one who saved her babe.::

For all its age, it sounded to Skyra like a lost child who wanted only to go home again.

I fear your home is also lost, lost to time.

::I know. But the Beloved's spirit is immortal. She is somewhere.::

"Would that we could help in that searching." Kirstine squeezed Skyra's hand. "But where even to start?"

::I felt the goddess near you both when you first met. I had hoped that you were halves of her spirit separated from each other, so I led you to each other again. But no. I am lost.::

Skyra mused on the coin's words and found an answer in the reflection of herself in Kirstine's eyes. *How do you know that we are not fragments or memories of her spirit? Mayhap you did what you were meant to do — you brought us together.*

The room brightened as if storm clouds had blown away from the sun. Kirstine looked at Skyra with eyes newly shining and added her thoughts. *I was a tethered bird, and Skyra has shown me I have it in me to fly. I always thought life should have more than I felt, and then you brought me to her, and then her to me.*

::I wanted the Green Woman saved. Ignorance and darkness always come for the women who have light.::

Kirstine lifted the coin from Skyra's palm as if she was handling the most delicate of flowers. *Will you finally tell me your name, little one?*

The coin's voice was fainter now, but Skyra could still hear it admit, ::I don't have a name. I am a nomisma. A coin, that is all.::

I think there is more to you than that. Let Nomisma be your name.::

::But it is not my name. I thank you, however.::

I am glad to understand you better.

::I will think on what you have said. It is good to be useful in the service of love.::

There can be no finer purpose.

With the coin on the table between them, Kirstine took hold of both Skyra's hands. "Thank you. Thank you for helping me bear this awful uncertainty."

"Of course."

Of course.

::Of course.::

They both picked up their tea as the sitting room door opened.

"I had to leave my horse up the road," Lachlann announced. "It is chaos out there now. Do you think it news of Androw?"

"I feel it in my heart," Kirstine said. "While I pray it is not my son."

"As do I." He gave Skyra a weary glance. The ride from the castle couldn't have been easy if the road was swelled with folk eager to hear what the news might be. "Might I have a moment with my sister?"

"Lachie," Kirstine said carefully. "She can hear our words. She has all my trust, surely as if she were another sister."

::We are all sisters.::

He sat down in the only remaining chair and shook his head when Kirstine lifted the teapot.

"I can go," Skyra offered, though she had no intention of doing so unless Kirstine asked.

"No. I need you. Stay. What would you say, Lachie?"

"If it is him, then everything changes."

"I know. If the black banner flies for both of them, then you must ride tonight to fetch Galdring from fosterage. If it is only Androw, then there is a little more time to bring him home to replace me and become his brother's steward. If Cannmor himself is bringing us the news of his father's death, then..."

"Catastrophe for you and me." His voice pitched very low, Lachlann finished, "Neither of us is his preferred counselor. I will go to my holdings, no doubt, and be a country farmer."

Kirstine's gaze was fixed on her cup. "I have no holdings to go to. No home to return to. When Cannmor marries, I'll have no rooms to call my own. These past twenty years leave me bankrupt."

"You will live with me," he declared. "I've not spent near enough time making the house there agreeable. We will make it so together." Quietly, his voice talking on a lilting accent, he added, "Maybe your grandchildren will visit, and we'll sing in the old tongue."

Skyra's heart thumped painfully, and she schooled herself to hide the twisting pain. His offer was a safe sanctuary. And it meant an end to them.

"Lachie, you need a wife, not a sister."

"You are the finest woman I know, Kirsty. I cannot replace the family the sea took from me."

"You are yet young for fatherhood. You can begin again, and you should have long since."

His face split into a rakish smile. "I could marry Skyra here. Think of the babes! As deadly as they would be beautiful."

Matching his tone, Skyra said, "I think not, my lord. I am pledged to the way of my axe." And my axe is pledged to her, she added to herself.

Kirstine smoothly suggested, "Mayhap we are speculating for nothing. It could be the Norse or Scot king, even the English one, or the kirk's lord — their Pope. It need not be catastrophe."

Kirstine didn't say it as if she believed it, however.

They returned to the pier to find it occupied beyond capacity. Soldiers Lachlann had ordered to follow after him finally arrived and set about pushing onlookers back onto the road. The three of them were able to make their way to the pier's edge where the Port Master was attempting to keep order.

Kirstine was buffered from the pushing and shoving by the weight of Lachlann's and Skyra's bodies. She stood still and quiet as the wide ship drew nearer, nearly all sails down for its final approach. The black banner and the flag of Clan Drummoch snapped in the sharp wind. Men on its deck began to shout the news, but the words were too faint.

"Is that Cannmor," Kirstine asked suddenly. "At the bow? Lachie can you tell?"

Lachlann shaded his eyes. "I think it is. There is no sign of Androw."

The Port Master lowered his sighting glass and agreed. "I see no sign of Lord Androw, but that's his heir." He recovered himself and said with genuine sympathy. "Lady, I am sorry."

Her voice steady and cool, Kirstine answered, "Thank you. You will need to clear this area for the new lord to come home."

The Port Master looked again at the approaching ship. "A bonny lady stands aside him."

Kirstine's breath caught though she made no sound.

Skyra murmured, "So it's catastrophe?"

Lachlann gave a mirthless laugh. "Worse than, if that's a bride. Courage, Sister."

I will not look ahead, Skyra told herself, though she could hear only the sound of crashing waves and the rending of iron on bitter rocks.

Chapter Twenty-Three

Kirstine watched her new daughter-by-law flutter her lashes at the son she no longer recognized.

Chin down, head turned, eyes lowered, she cooed, "As my lord wishes" to his every request.

She shows her neck like prey, and it makes him feel like a lion.

::Can you do that?::

Not for long.

Catastrophe, complete catastrophe. Horses had been found for Cannmor and his bride Liesel, and the two led the slow procession homeward. Behind them came the wagon carrying Androw's bier. The sun had reached its long summer twilight, allowing Androw's people to line the road in somber honor to their dead and living lords. Cannmor, so like his father in dark hair and beard, received calls of fealty and well wishes as his due.

Kirstine was numb to all but her despairing anger. Lachie and Skyra rode to either side of her, as silent and stone faced as she was. Let the world take it for grief.

Cannmor had set foot on the pier and embraced her. In the next breath he introduced the new Lady of Castle Drummoch and gave Kirstine leave to take the night to plan how to vacate the rooms she occupied.

She had met the dagger eyes of her new daughter-by-law without flinching and sweetly said, "I wish you the same welcome and joy that I have known these twenty years."

She wanted to be held in Skyra's arms. To rage and weep. But her only choice was to play her part in what was now her son's story.

They finally reached the castle, and Kirstine could see that Lachie's soldiers had carried the news quick enough that much of the household staff, including the Seal Keeper Benneit and clever Una, was lined up to greet their new lord and lady. Kirstine slipped away with Skyra following behind her. She wanted only to be alone now, before she broke.

It seemed the castle had emptied, for they met no one until the top of the stairs where Marial sat half weeping on her bed. She sprang up at Kirstine's approach.

"Lady, can I do anything for you? I am so sorry. Such terrible news."

"I am fine, Marial, but I am afraid for you. I am leaving these rooms on the morrow."

"So soon?"

Kirstine knew her attempt at a calming smile failed. "I hope I can still accommodate your service, but—"

Marial took her hands and held them to her chest. "Do not worry about me, Lady. I have had no chance to tell you that yesterday Blond Bruce, the miller's eldest son, offered for me."

"Marial, this is wonderful news." And it was. Some of the weight lifted from Kirstine's heavy heart. "You care for him and he for you?"

"Yes. And he has promised that I will teach our sons and daughters to read and number as you taught me. Bruce says we will have need for learned children. He thinks there are means to build a second wheel upstream. I think that would — I'm sorry." Her young face filled with concern. "You look so tired, and your heart must be so sore."

"Your news has brightened this awful day." She was glad, indeed, that Marial's kind soul had found a place of her own. "But yes, I am tired. I want nothing but to sleep now. Send away all that you can. I could sleep for a week, though I'll not have that luxury."

A polite cough behind them made Kirstine aware that the unmistakable wide form of her kitchen steward was in the doorway and breathing hard under the weight of a wide, covered platter.

"What is this?"

"The condolences of the staff, Lady. You must be famished and will not have thought to have care for yourself."

Touched, she stood aside so the woman could carry the platter into the sitting room. "I thank you. Please tell all the staff, every one of them, that I am grateful." Before the steward could begin one of her long rambles, she added, "Have you heard that Marial is to be wed? Take her down with you and find some morsel of cake to celebrate."

She bade them goodbye and closed the antechamber door to the continuing bustle in the stair and hall as Cannmor's trunks were carried up. Moments later she was locking her own door behind her. Her own door for one more night.

Skyra had been standing at the open doors to the Lady's Watch and looking across the bailey toward the paddock. She left off to set her axe in its usual place but didn't remove her armor as she usually did when the door was locked. No doubt she presumed that they would be interrupted.

Kirstine held out her hand and they sat in chairs at the fire as they always did. Skyra uncovered the platter to reveal a half loaf of bread, a joint of meat, toasted chestnuts, and a crock of the tangy goat cheese that they both loved.

"I'm hungry," she admitted.

Skyra was already carving off slices of meat. "That's a good thing. It's hard to be numb and hungry at the same time."

Kirstine set about slicing the bread. "Did you make any sense of his explanation? About Androw?"

"Only that it was a wasting illness, and he was gone in a week."

"He fell ill at the Norse king's court. He was the only one who did. Odd, that."

Skyra's tone was dry as she echoed, "Very odd. I could not hear what else he said. About the wedding."

She bit off a piece of the meat Skyra offered her and followed it with a chunk of the bread. Her hunger abated, and she felt on steadier ground. "The Norse king was so grieved by Androw's death that he offered to send his brother to ensure that Androw's lands were held safe while Cannmor continued to the crusade. I will give my son credit for refusing that offer."

"Because he might have fallen ill himself soon after? Or faced an accident on the way to the Holy Land?"

"Indeed. I don't think anyone expected him to agree because the marriage was offered so quickly instead. A thin alliance through even thinner blood to the Norse king himself."

"What will we do?"

Skyra's voice was low and seemingly calm, but Kirstine could sense the tension and anguish.

"I am thinking on it."

"Your brother's offer is generous."

"If he were all I had, I would gladly go. But I have you, and I will not be parted."

"I would not leave you." Skyra's voice broke. "But I have nothing to offer you."

"You are everything."

"Sing for me," Skyra said. "When you are able. The song you told me earlier you wanted to."

"The day began so brightly." Mind made up, she added, "I won't let it end this way. I'll sing."

They sat quietly and ate for a few more minutes.

"It's a lament," Kirstine finally said. She wiped her fingers on the linen napkin. "In the language of my home."

Skyra had gone to fetch her harp. She put her dagger and the coin on the table and left her cloak on the chair.

"Bring it to the Lady's Watch. No one here will know the words, but all will understand the music."

Chapter Twenty-Four

Whenever Kirstine decided to sing on the Lady's Watch, Skyra always stepped into the darkness just inside the door. A lamp on the table at her side illuminated Kirstine's face, and the vantage gave Skyra leave to watch Kirstine's long, supple fingers at play on the strings.

She would do so again tonight, though her world was teetering on the edge of ruin. There was no place for them here – gone in the blink of an eye. This son, Cannmor, had none of Kirstine in him that Skyra could see. He strongly reminded her of the angry leader of the men who'd attacked Breda. Aspiration ate at him. He would never be satisfied and everyone in his sight would be to blame. Even if Kirstine stayed, she wouldn't be safe from his spite or his bride's calculating eyes.

As Kirstine tuned the strings the bailey below them quieted as it usually did when word was passed that there would be music from the Lady's Watch. Skyra was, as always, amused at the winces and frowns that crossed Kirstine's face as she listened and adjusted the strings.

At last the frowns were gone, and Kirstine said in her cool, clear voice, "This is called 'The Lament of Egrid.' It's a story of love and brave hope."

The first notes were wistful and accompanied by Kirstine's low hum. Skyra did not need to know the language to understand a call to sit and hear a story, to prepare for tears and sighs. The wistful quality grew stronger, and into the melody came a bold hero's declaration. Of love — it had to be of love — but Kirstine had called it a lament. If it were love, it would fail.

Kirstine was weaving magic as she always did, but Skyra could only hear the lowest notes, plucked continuously as a droning counterpoint. Her heartbeat began to pound in her ears, and she found herself on the floor.

Kirstine was almost within reach, but the red memory was between them.

She had smelled blood in her dreams all through the months. At Breda's she'd scraped caked flecks of it from the carvings on her axe. There was so much blood, brown and red, drying in the sun. Someone close by was retching. Near and far were cries of the wounded.

The low drone from the harp carried her across the field to where opposing sides now stood with weapons sheathed. The Karl of Stane stood face-to-face with his cousin. As she watched in growing disbelief on the bloody field of the dead and dying, they shared the kiss of peace and laughed.

They had both called their soldiers to battle for the sake of honor. A woman defiled, a ship raided, an inheritance stolen. Tavern fights escalated into this field of war. She was soaked with blood. The faces of the dead, her dead, drifted past her eyes. Children orphaned, women made widow.

And they *laughed.*

"For this? Did I make this field of blood and death so they could laugh?"

In a place where the light reached, nowhere near her, she could hear the clear power of Kirstine's voice, raised in brave hope. She was too far away to lift shame from Skyra's spirit. Too far away to set her past to right.

::It can't be set right.::

I am covered in blood.

::Only the future can ease the past. The future is through the next door, and the one after.::

I am covered in blood.

::Open your eyes.::

She was still there, Kirstine in the lamplight, in the moonlight, with her dark eyes lit by stars and a voice calling for love to stay in spite of the shame and grief.

Kirstine's voice fell silent, and her fingers stilled. The harp strings still vibrated with their final note, and in that quiet moment all the rest of it came. Who she had been. The faces of her parents, so proud to send their daughter to serve their Karl. The smiles of the women, kind and sweet, who'd shared in her desires and brought her peace.

Her comrades-in-arms lying dead in mud made red by senseless war.

She'd thrown down her colors and her rank. Walked away, and walked farther, walked away from her name, her land, and her people. She waited for passage to another shore and out of the dark came the cracking blow to her head. Then only a thick gray of gasping pain.

Finally, Breda's dark face was before her, in concern and kindness, then she faded away to the sound of Kirstine's delighted laughter on the night that had set her on this path.

There was something else to know. There had been a skirmish with angry men, stupid men, who meant to harm Breda.

She had been filled with battle fury, but she hadn't killed them. That much she could take comfort in.

"My love," Kirstine was saying. "Come back."

Her head was in Kirstine's lap and the lavender scent of her gown was all around her. The tang of blood faded, but not completely.

"You've remembered?"

"Yes."

"Is it bad?"

"I killed. I killed so many, and for nothing. In the service of a lord who would only look for peace after playing a game in blood shed by others."

Kirstine's gentle fingers stroked her forehead. "Many have made that mistake. Do you want to tell me?"

She did, and the telling was brief. She felt Kirstine sigh, though her gentle touch never faltered. "Your song brought me back like a beacon. And the coin too."

"I didn't think that old song had such power. It was the first I learned, though I've changed the music since. It is not so sad, is it, to hope for love?"

She pulled Kirstine's fingers to her lips. "Sing it again for me sometime?"

"Of course. But it won't be on Midsummer, not here. You and I will be gone by then."

Chapter Twenty-Five

"But this is madness, Kirsty. You don't even know if your daughter will make you welcome."

Lachie's support was essential to her plans. "Gunnhild wrote that she is with child again and asked, now that I am widowed, if I might visit. She offers me a place where I can be useful and honored."

The three of them had ridden to the hill near the port. In the distance the sea rolled sleepily in the summer warmth. Nearer, the port was crowded with merchant ships and fishing vessels. Kirstine put aside her habit of estimating the food each might carry and how many it might feed. She was not here to do that.

She had brought her sharp-eyed brother here to lie to him.

"You are useful and honored here."

Skyra snorted and badly feigned a cough to cover it.

"Useful, yes. Liesel has made it very clear that, since I know how, I can plan Midsummer and Lammas, and all the rest, including the innumerable feast days of that god she loves so much. And I can go on counting the grain yields and sheep and deciding on the storage levels for winter. And to increase the food allotment for the royal family because sharing sacrifice equally is not what her god requires of her. All this she will *allow* me to do, out of kindness."

"You don't find honor in that?"

"Would you? To labor without reward so another can shine?"

"You did it for Androw."

"His ring was on my finger. A contract was struck." Cannmor had already spoken of disrupting the trade to the west at the Norse king's bidding. Drummoch ships would no doubt encounter those of Galrandel. Just as water was wet, the peace bought by twenty years of her life was over.

The only happy result of the upheaval was that Galdring would at least stay where he was, happy in fosterage. His heart had never yearned for the lord's chair.

Skyra had wandered some distance along the crest. Kirstine left off her argument with Lachie to watch the wind lift the long red hair. The pain of not knowing her past had been replaced by the pain of knowing it, but it was an easier pain.

In the small room they now shared she could reach from her narrow bed to Skyra's and gentle her dreams. Quiet kisses made the days bearable, but the room had no lock and all but the briefest of intimacies had to wait.

She was telling Lachie a truth to hide the lie. Gunnhild was indeed with child but asked for Kirstine's presence at the lying-in, seven months hence. She had written back to agree, also saying she was going home for the autumn, now that she had the time to do so.

She would be in neither place, and those who cared — Lachie at least — wouldn't realize for months that she was gone. By then she and Skyra would be completely elsewhere, into the wild lands at the farthest reach of kings and kirks.

"How will we not be found?" Skyra had asked.

"We'll travel the Green Women's road. I'd not involve Breda, for that is the first place Lachie would go. But you can speak of knowing her, and I believe women like her will guide us onward."

"We will be together."

"Mayhap we will find a place to be useful and safe." She had kissed Skyra then, in needful silence.

She asked Lachlann now, "Do you remember the first winter we spent here? When the old ones and babies died for want of food, and no one seemed to care?"

"I do."

"That winter is coming again. There is a dark wind that I cannot sail into. Cannmor listens to you, for now. Find happiness, Brother, and hold it close."

He left off patting the neck of her mare to give her an accusing look. "You're not coming back."

This was the hardest lie, the one he wouldn't forgive.

She wanted to tell him the truth, but he would repeat his offer of refuge. Any future must include Skyra. Much as she loved Lachie, she didn't believe he could fathom that she was the sovereign of her own body and future, and she had the right to give her heart to a woman. "I will, in time. All I need of you is the horses, and I'd be grateful for a small purse and your love. Gunnhild will provide me with all else."

"Of course you shall have all, but I still don't understand." He called to Skyra, "Will you allow this madness?"

Skyra gigged her bay toward them again, and when close enough to answer without shouting, she said, "You ask me that as if your sister would need my permission."

"Have you nothing to say?"

"My memory has come back."

Lachie sighed hard and Kirstine committed his handsome, worried face to memory. "So you are going home."

"No, I am going with her." Skyra's gaze met Kirstine's. "To my ending."

"I take comfort in that."

Kirstine's heartache eased. Her beloved brother would not worry, at least at first.

"You believe me, that I will never leave her?"

"I know that she believes you." Again he sighed, this time with something like acceptance. "Does your axe have a name after all?"

Kirstine listened with interest as Skyra nodded, for she had not thought to ask this question.

"She is *Beri Longu Natten*, Bringer of the Long Night, and belonged to my mother. My mother called her a labrys."

"So there *are* more of you. Heaven help us."

"There were, at least. You are safe from warrior women. For now."

Chapter Twenty-Six

Kirstine had not wanted a farewell, and so there wasn't one. Why bother, she dissembled, when her absence was temporary? There was no need to bring more than they could carry for such a short journey, was there?

After assuring himself that Kirstine's mare was properly ready, Captain Egann brought her hand to his forehead with a deep bow. Lachie, with a smile that didn't hide his sadness, helped her mount that last time.

Skyra was already astride her bay, of course. They both had heavy saddlebags, even though the contents were only the barest of essentials. Under her kirtle Kirstine had tied the purse of gold coin Lachie had given her. Her talisman coin she kept tucked in her bodice. Her harp rested in a leather sling across her back in its oiled wrappers. The beautiful inlay box that had held it all these years she had given to Marial as a wedding gift.

Nothing could change her mind about leaving, but she was nonetheless afraid they would not get far enough away, and quickly enough, to disappear into the anonymity of northern tribes. Skyra believed, even though conditions were likely to be harsh, that women there were allowed some freedom to choose their own way.

::*If we are near the energy of the goddess, I will know.*::

We would be grateful for that. It's a long road ahead. Knowing those we can call friend will help.

In the quiet of the summer's early dawn, they rode through the castle gates together. Kirstine put her gloved hand to her lips and cast a final wave to Lachie.

"I'm sorry," Skyra said. "I'll miss him too."

She cried a little then, and they pressed forward. By midday they dined lightly at an inn Captain Egann had said was a good midpoint. By afternoon they reached the crossroads where forward lay the road to Gunnhild's clan, and north led to a small port where a ferry would take them to the nearest island.

Other travelers on the road might recall two women, one with a harp, the other with an axe, turning toward the ferry. It would be weeks, possibly months, however, before anyone asked. Their next step would depend on what the Green Woman on the island told them.

Long past sunset, in sight of the small port, they came finally to an inn. The door was not yet locked, and the sleepy innkeeper was glad to let an empty room. Weary to her bones, Kirstine carried up the saddlebags while Skyra saw to the horses. There was one wide bed, and it was marvelous in Kirstine's eyes.

By the time Skyra arrived, Kirstine was in her sleeping gown, and doing her best to warm the cold sheets. Her hair was loose around her shoulders the way Skyra loved. She thought she might not ever bind it into a braid again.

"You are a wondrous sight," Skyra said. She set their saddlebags against the door and began piling her armor on them as well. Her fingers were quick on her laces, and in moments she joined Kirstine in the bed.

"Put out the candle," she murmured with a kiss in that wild soft place behind Kirstine's ear.

"Not yet. There is one thing I would ask you first."

With a fire of hunger in her eyes, Skyra said, "Ask, then."

She drew a long strip of white cloth from under her gown and picked up her dagger. She set both in front of them on the blankets.

Skyra's breath quickened. "Do you mean it?"

"With all my heart. We will never be parted, I swear it."

::Never parted. This is the promise that matters.::

"Yes, then." Without further hesitation, Skyra picked up the dagger and drew a long shallow line across her palm. "I will not regret this blood."

Kirstine drew a similar line on her own palm, avoiding the one she made so many years ago on her wedding day. Her *first* wedding day, she amended. Today was her second. There would be no more.

Their palms pressed together, blood to blood, they took turns in the ritual winding of the cloth to complete the handfasting.

Kirstine had no wish to repeat the ritual words she'd said long ago that had sealed a contract, not a life. Instead, she spoke from the depths of her belief in their future. "You are and will always be a knight to me. My knight for all my nights and days, of my body and my heart."

"Oh my love." Skyra pale eyes were bright with tears and the reflection from the candle. "You are and will always be my lady."

Kirstine moved to cup Skyra's face with her hands and realized that it was, of course, now awkward to do with their hands bound.

"It seems to me," Skyra said then, "that I had plans for my hands that won't be possible until the morning."

"Oh." Kirstine had to laugh at herself. "As did I. Mayhap this could have waited until after, but I could not think how we would relight the candle."

"I am glad you didn't wait." Skyra kissed the back of the cloth on Kirstine's hand. "Sleep is welcome too."

"I propose we see what our other hands might be capable of." Kirstine's free hand found its way between them. "Or are you too weary?"

"No, not at all. I'd forgotten for a moment how inventive you are."

"And now?"

"Blow out the candle, my love."

This time, she did.

The End

The first time I was lost, the mountain fire tried to reclaim me. She who held me cast me into the sea of her endless grief.

I have learned that I know when the essence of the Beloved is near. The old magic rose in me. In the goddess's wisdom, two hearts united, and in time to escape the darkness that always comes for women with light of their own.

Now I realize my purpose — to cherish these fragments of the love not yet bloomed and urge it toward its mate.

I will be useful in the service of love. There is no higher calling.

My journey begins again and will continue until I rest once more in the Beloved's hand.

A Millennia of Music - Playlist

Plainchant. Harps, fiddles, and pipes. Drum circles. This playlist is a sampling across two of the traditions in medieval music we can hear today. One is historically accurate with instruments made as closely as possible to how they would have been in the medieval era. The other is current performances using the descendants of those instruments and motifs to tell stories, whip up a dance, or soothe the restless spirit.

You can hear this 80-minute playlist at Spotify. Search for me as "Shades of Karin" and look for *Knight of Nights*.

* * *

Orzchis: Written by Jocelyn Montgomery and arranged by David Lynch based on writings by Hildegard von Bingen.

An Eala Bhàn (The White Swan): Composed by Dòmhnall Ruadh Chorùna. Artists: Julie Fowlis, Muireann Nic Amhlaoibh, Eamon Doorley, Ross Martin.

Ormagardskvedi (Snake Pit Poetry): Derived from the *Tale of Ragnor Lodbrok*, 13th Century. Artist: Wardruna.

Huron "Beltane" Fire Dance: Written and performed by Loreena McKennitt.

Banquet Hall: Written and performed by Loreena McKennitt.

In the Merry Month of May: Traditional. Performed by Patricia Spero.

The Wind that Shakes the Barley: Written and performed by Dead Can Dance (Lisa Gerrard and Brendan Perry).

Orbis de Ignis: Written and performed by Dead Can Dance.

The Mystic's Dream: Written and performed by Loreena McKennitt.

Zachaeus Arboris (Benedicamen): Traditional prayer. Performed by Schola Hungarica, László Dobszay, Janka Szendrei.

Kyrie Eleison: Traditional prayer. Performed and engineered by Stellamara.

Chant of the Paladin: Written and performed by Dead Can Dance.

The Lady of Shalott: Text by Alfred Tennyson. Adapted and performed by Loreena McKennitt. While the text was written long after the medieval era, the romantic, sad tale was much like those sung by bards in medieval halls.

Vision 1 "The Fire of Creation" - Et Ego Homo: Written by Hildegard von Bingen. Performed by Anonymous 4.

O Virtus Sapientiae for Cello and Orchestra: Written by Hildegard von Bingen. Performed by Raphaela Gromes, Lucerne Festival Strings, Daniel Dodds.

I Asked for Love: Written and performed by Lisa Gerrard and Patrick Cassidy.

Pearl: Composed and arranged by Katharine Blake. Performed by Mediæval Bæbes.

Valborgsbål: Written and performed by Magnus Ek and Raun.

May the Circle Be Open (Chants of the Ancient Mother): Written by Robert Gass. Arrangement and choir direction by Jane Howard.

Theme from Harry's Game: Written by Pól Brennan and Ciarán Brennan. Performed by Pól Brennan, Ciarán Brennan, Voces8, Gareth McLearnon.

Battle and Aftermath: Written by Jocelyn Montgomery and arranged by David Lynch. Not so much a song as an evocation of a cold, windy battlefield.

Notes on the World of *Knight of Nights*

Do You Really Want to Know How It Really Was?

Writers walk a perilous tightrope in historical fiction. Verisimilitude – the appearance of being true or real – is essential. However, some of the daily realities in historical eras are unappealing. For example, it probably smelled. Smelled *bad*. The food in climates without year-round growing seasons was probably flavorless and oversalted. Most people had bad teeth and foul breaths. Those aren't the realities I chose to dwell on for long in this story.

Hunger was commonplace in medieval times. The gift of a meal could be, literally, lifesaving. As was the gift of a fire – in climates far from the equator, it was relentlessly cold for most of the year. There was also no aspirin or ibuprofen. Everyone, including children, drank mild ale throughout the day. It was often cleaner than water. That's right – everyone in olden times was getting through the day partially buzzed.

Religious superstition filled in the blanks that science hadn't yet explained. In this story, the scientists are what I've called Green Women. Historically, these women (and sometimes men) lived isolated lives connected to natural science. This plant healed, that one killed, these crops grown together increased the health of both. These naturalists were often Druidic or Pagan in practice, but not all. Regardless of their traditions, these women were eventually hunted as witches, a reality I wrote about in my novel *Christabel*.

When, Where, and Why

This story is set in a time of invention and change as northern European cultures practiced repetitive conquest on their neighbors and stayed to intermarry. Languages and rites merged, and the mythos and power structures of Christianity usurped pagan practice and myth. In this part of the world, Beltane was not yet Easter, but suspicion of science was rising.

It was difficult to decide exactly when to set this story in what was a prolonged, tumultuous period. History is blurred by fictions, some a thousand years old. Today, some movies treat anything from Arthurian legend to *Braveheart* as the same era and geography when they are at least 500 years and 500 miles apart.

I finally decided to loosely anchor it to the time of the Norse Crusade and the general region of northeast Scotland and near island cultures. It is difficult to pinpoint when certain inventions — such as armor made of chain link versus scales of metal stitched to stiff leather — came into being. It is equally impossible to pinpoint when that invention reached local use.

When I had to choose, I leaned toward the description or practice that I thought most readers would already know of or expect to see. Without, I hope, getting it terribly wrong.

What's in a Name?

The melting pot/culture clash in this part of the world is easy to see in the evolution of languages. From their shared Celtic roots, Irish, Manx, and Cornish danced the do-si-do for hundreds of years through trade and marriage. Welsh and Scottish Gaelic kept most of their own style, but Pictish and others were subsumed or disappeared. Old Norse was constantly declaring new dance-offs with a simple rule: Winner Gets All the Stuff and It's Our Way Now. Flemish, Breton, and other settlers moved into the region to cement a new regime's administration.

Now take all of that fusion and have each in turn discarded, modified, or restored in small areas, coming from all directions, for a couple of hundred years. The last bit of chaos? Official proceedings, like a census or court laws and rulings, were written down in Latin.

After a generation with one language (and sacred practices, basic rights, specific rules of inheritance, et al), a new dude with a crew would be interested in some local resource or bragging rights and take over by brute force. If no tight relation to his new subjects, he'd impose another language variant, sacred practices, basic rights, and so on. The local populace resisted, adapted, and got on with surviving the icy weather, bad food, and rampant disease.

The European Dark and Middle Ages rubbed shoulders for more than a hundred years. From generation to generation a MacDonald might be a Donaldson and back again. Surnames were a matter of convenience and not legally recorded until the late 1200s. And then they were probably written in Latin. Welcome *Donalicus*...

As a pitiful monolingual American choosing names for this story, I used common roots and eased the spelling toward phonetic pronunciation while keeping a sense of the heritage — mostly Irish or Norse — behind it.

As Always, Women Adapt

During this endless upheaval, women adapted. What choice did they have? One moment they could own land, the next they couldn't. One moment they were revered and respected as mothers of their families and elders of their clan, the next they were responsible for all sin. A leader could be feared as Asta Bloodaxe or reduced to "and wife." *Knight of Nights* is set at the changing of one such tide.

If you're thinking there are modern parallels to this distant history, you're not wrong. Science is once again declaimed as treasonous when it is inconvenient or a threat to power. Cultural upheaval and fusion are spurring violence from those who fear that change will disrupt their right to behave any way they want regardless of the harm it visits on others.

In these interesting times, love remains the only true ship that can sail against these dark winds.

— *Karin Kallmaker, 2023*

Acknowledgments

I am deeply grateful for the patience of Heather Flournoy in editing this story, and for the social media communities who take one look at a woman in armor and go "ooo." Thank you, *Vanity Fair*, for putting Emma Thompson in full armor on your February 1996 cover. (Don't know it? A web image search will find it for you. You're welcome.) I think this story — and the cover — have been cooking in my brain ever since.

Thank you for letting me tell you this story!

When you purchase from the publisher or author more of your dollars reach the women who write and produce the books you love. About you, for you. Your support and the word of mouth you spread with reviews means everything.

Print, eBook, and audio versions of novels, plus many digital short stories, are available from Bella Books and the usual major online retailers. Signed print copies, background information, and additional digital short stories — including free reads — are available at Kallmaker.com.

Please connect with me in the way that works for you. You can find me on Facebook, Mastodon, Twitter, or you can visit my blog, *Romance and Chocolate*, at Kallmaker.com. Search for "Kallmaker" — there's only one. Which is probably for the best.

Scan the QR Code to sign up for
Karin's Private Newsletter

It's private: Karin or a trusted helper are the only people with access to it. Emails and her site are *ad-free*.

It's treasured: It will never be given away, shared, or sold.

It's to the point: It will be used infrequently and only to let you know specifically about the availability of Karin's writing. Fewer than 12 ad-free emails a year.

It's your choice: Unsubscribe at any time. We don't keep track and won't be offended. Your mailbox is your business.

Sample from Book One:
Velvet in Venice

I begin.

Made in fire and hammered to life, I was born in the shadow of Mons Mykali. My molten heart was cooled in the sacred spring that flows to the Icarian Sea.

I was made for the Beloved to mark the beginning of Forever, as granted by Aphaea Artemis, she of wisdom and compassion for all that endures. I am the promise between two equal spirits.

Three millennia have I flowed from hand to hand to find the Beloved again. I have found many beloveds, but not her whom Aphaea Artemis blessed, and in whose hand I will rest again.

I breathe fire into one who hides her heart behind walls of marble.

EXCERPT FROM
CHAPTER ONE

A few euros would buy Artie a lite meal in the casino's ristorante and gift shop, and she knew where to sit that was close enough to hear the music from the cabaret. Both were located at the courtyard entrance to the historic casino building. She'd been in the casino as a tour guide, of course, but its opulence and intense high-roller, high-money atmosphere was not for the likes of her otherwise.

The more casual courtyard would be the perfect respite from the heat, along with the "piatto da cucina" she knew to ask for. The kitchen's daily special of bread and sliced meats, with fresh figs or sliced pear, was plated for locals only, with a price lower than any dish on the printed menu.

She exchanged a friendly wink with the server who tended the wine bar, whose company had been welcome until breakfast once, but with no strings whatsoever. There was a hint of interest in Giorgia's eyes for later tonight, but it was simply too hot. Artie declined with a minute ripple of fingers — one of those ineffable Italian gestures that summarized an entire conversation of pleasantries.

She ate the meal slowly, stretching out her time in air-conditioning as long as possible.

The little ristorante was crowded with a waiting line by the time she finished the last of the figs and drained a second glass of chilled sparkling water. It was time to go. She settled her bill and made her way to the covered courtyard, mentally girding herself to go out into the sun again.

As Artie settled her satchel along the front of her torso, she heard fresh music coming from the Casino di Venezia cabaret. The prime of the evening had been occupied by an eternally popular ABBA tribute act that had made her meal all the more pleasant. This music was a softer, bluesier sound that was purely American. Or sounded so to her ears.

Beguiled by the unexpected melody, she decided she could afford the glass of wine it would cost her to listen. She realized she was homesick, something she hadn't thought possible.

The moment she crossed the threshold into the cabaret, her gaze was drawn to the vocalist. Her dark brown skin shimmered with red highlights in the stage lights. A glittering blue dress wrapped around her shapely, ample body to frame broad shoulders. Dark gold cornrows ended in neon orange, lime, and raspberry beads that sparkled as she swayed to the music she made. Her hands danced over the keyboard as her voice rippled like cool water on marble stones.

Artie found a seat at a tiny table without taking her gaze off the singer's face. Thick, red lips nearly brushed the microphone in front of her. Large, dark eyes widened and flashed as the melody rose and fell.

It took a moment for Artie to realize that the woman was singing "Take Me Home, Country Roads." The transformation into a minor key filled the words with longing and loneliness. It seemed an odd piece for a casino cabaret, but it segued seamlessly into a more upbeat "Walking in Memphis." By the third piece the singer had fully hit her stride with a saucy, sultry rendition of "Route 66."

Artie was sorry when the set ended. There was no way she could stay for the woman's next set at eleven o'clock. She had a tour tomorrow morning and ought to be home trying to sleep by then. The cantante had a full, sensuous figure, though, and her parting smile was lively and genuine — and abruptly very tempting.

Another hour spent gazing at it while under the spell of that lush voice would be restorative, a small voice inside argued. But the prospect of an early morning followed by kilometers of walking after only a few hours' sleep was dismal enough to have her regretfully leaving a five-euro note in the jar on the piano and walking home at last.

The heat of the day had diminished to a tolerable level. The expected breeze had come up as well, making the fifteen-minute walk to her apartment on the Rio Terà dei Biri almost pleasant.

The family on the second floor, also her landlords, had had grilled fish and polenta on their balcony, or at least it smelled like that had been dinner. The children were still playing a game on the landing and called, "Ciao, Artie!" as she passed them on her way to the third floor and its only door.

Her apartment was a large, undivided attic room, save for the water closet in one corner, and she had thought it best not to ask if the owners had ever gotten the necessary permits for the heat and running water. Permits in Venice — it was a can of worms only a fool would open.

"Don't forget Winona, Kingman, Barstow..." She dropped ice cubes from the tray in her tiny freezer into chilled sparkling water from the bottle in the icebox. Ice was a luxury, and she didn't take it for granted.

She woo-woo-woo'd her way from the utilitarian kitchen to the comfortable sofa that had been in the apartment when she'd arrived and would still be here when she left. Nobody moved furniture in Venice if it could be avoided.

Sitting down, legs stretched out onto the coffee table, felt wonderful. After a half hour spent on her laptop confirming and updating tour bookings, she was in a surprisingly good mood and decided on a cool bath before bed.

She emptied her pockets onto the bureau next to the bed. They were full of the usual things from a day of touring — receipts for tickets, a gum wrapper, loose change, and a coil of folding money that had been tips from the group.

She tucked the bills into the back of the top drawer to go toward the rent. The rent had become all the more reasonable when she'd offered to pay in cash. A little more cash than that had purchased her landlord's Wi-Fi password.

As she scooped the coins into her change bowl, she realized that one she'd thought was a two euro at the bodega wasn't ringed in silver. She looked more closely but couldn't make out the country of origin.

The face of the coin featured two figureheads, bent close together as if conferring. It was quite old and rubbed shiny across the faces of the figures. It was possibly worth more than two euros.

In better light she might be able to discern its origins. She'd take it to the library the next time she went, maybe, and use one of the magnifiers they had on hand for reading tiny scripts. In the meantime, she'd keep it on the bedside table. It was definitely intriguing.

Her skin cool and clean, she finally curled up in bed and fell asleep humming bars of "Route 66." In the morning the first thing she saw when she woke up was the coin, gleaming in the sunlight. It was so beautiful that she dropped it into the small, zippered pouch where she kept the key to her flat and headed out to the first tour of the day.

Velvet in Venice is available at all the usual retailers.
Visit Kallmaker.com for signed paperbacks.

Stories in the *Coin of Love Series*
can be read in any order.

Other Works by Karin Kallmaker

At www.Kallmaker.com you'll find excerpts, reviews, readings, free downloads and more. For a complete list of titles click on *All About Everything*.

Cowboys and Kisses

Abandoned in a small frontier town, Darlin' has no expectation of a long or happy life — until she sees a familiar longing in the gaze of a townswoman. *I Heart SapphFic Historical Romance of the Year* (Lesbian Historical Romance Short Novel)

Velvet in Venice

The allure of Venice keeps Artie Bryson happily buried in the past. Until the night Nikki Velvet's sultry voice lures Artie into the Casino di Venezia cabaret. And the night after that... *Coin of Love series Book One*. Stories in this series can be read in any order. (Lesbian Romance Novella)

Simply the Best

Cynical New York journalist Alice Cabot isn't about to succumb to the charms of California's beaches, fake Hollywood glamor, or simply perfect Pepper Addington. *Golden Crown Finalist* (Lesbian Romance - Fiction Novel)

Unbeliever

Love is magic is love. Hayley's life is complicated by a mysterious book of blank pages – and an alluring new neighbor who challenges everything Hayley doesn't believe in, including love. (Lesbian Romance Novella)

Because I Said So

Josie and Paz want to get married, but their respective guardians scoff at the very idea of love at first sight. So they arrange for Kesa and Shannon to meet. Nothing goes as planned... *Golden Crown Award Winner* (Lesbian Romance Novel)

My Lady Lipstick

Diana Beckinsale is the most alluring woman Paris Ellison has ever met, but Paris can't condone her madcap plans. Not when Diana is a completely different woman every time they meet. It's all fun and games until somebody loses her heart. *Golden Crown Award Winner* (Lesbian Romance Novel)

A Fish Out of Water

The 77th daughter of the Mer queen is irrevocably bound to a human woman by a deadly curse. Stripped of her voice, Ariel must find a way to save them both. (Lesbian Romance and Fantasy Novella inspired by *The Little Mermaid*)

Castle Wrath

When an ingénue inherits a remote, storm-drenched castle in a foreign land, she doesn't expect romance, sex, and intrigue as part of the inheritance. Or a curiously attractive caretaker. (Lesbian Romance Novella inspired by Jane Austen's *Northanger Abbey*)

Captain of Industry
What happens when passions get in the way of cherished dreams? Strong women like Jennifer Lamont and Suzanne Mason can have everything — except each other. *Golden Crown Finalist.* (Lesbian Romance Novel and companion to *Stepping Stone*)

Love by the Numbers
Dr. Nicole Hathaway needs an assistant. Down-on- her-luck socialite Lily Smith needs a job. Who cares if they hate each other on sight? *Lambda Literary Finalist.* (Lesbian Romance Novel)

Comfort and Joy
Home from Afghanistan to surprise her mother, Milla doesn't expect more than the best apple pie in the world and the bliss of unrationed hot showers. She's not counting on futures — or meeting a woman like Tyna. (Lesbian Romance Novella)

All the Wrong Places
A steamy look at sex and the single girl as Brandy weighs her free-for-all life against her growing feelings for her best friend. *Lambda Literary and Golden Crown Finalist.* (Lesbian Erotic Romance Novel)

Roller Coaster
Laura Izmani is glad of her new client, a wealthy actress who needs a private chef for her twins. She's also grateful that Helen Baynor doesn't remember their first meeting on a roller coaster ride that changed their lives. *Golden Crown Finalist.* (Sapphic Romance Novel)

Above Temptation
Kip Barrett does her job as a financial investigator very well, and nothing can tempt her from following the rules, not even her boss's boss's boss, Tamara Sterling. *Golden Crown Award Winner.* (Lesbian Intrigue- Romance Novel)

Stepping Stone
Hollywood Indie Producer Selena Ryan isn't going to let anyone use her to get what they want, ever again, even if that means living without love. *Lambda Literary Finalist.* (Lesbian Romance Novel)

The Kiss that Counted
CJ Roshe has finally met a woman she could love. If only she could tell Karita Hanssen her real name. *Lambda Literary and Golden Crown Award Winner.* (Lesbian Romance Novel)

Painted Moon - 25th Anniversary Edition
Stranded together in a snowbound cabin, Jackie Frakes and Leah Beck's lives will never be the same. The 25th Anniversary edition includes two additional short stories and a foreword by the author. (Lesbian Romance Novel)

Warming Trend
A river of ice has frozen Anidyr Bycall's life. The future looks even colder when she returns home to the glaciers of Alaska, the mistakes of her past and the disdain of the woman she once loved. (Lesbian Intrigue-Romance Novel)

Christabel
Can financier Dina Rowland and supermodel Christabel escape the cycle of doomed fate to conquer the past and

claim a future at last? A gothic tale of two hearts taken captive in colonial New York. (Lesbian Gothic Romance Novel)

Wild Things

Dutiful daughter Faith Fitzgerald has met the perfect man. There's just one problem: she's in love with his sister. (Lesbian Romance Novel)

In Deep Waters: Cruising the Seas

Karin Kallmaker and Radclyffe can't wait to get you all wet with this dual erotic short story collection. *Golden Crown Literary Award Winner.* (Lesbian Erotic Short Story Collection)

Car Pool

Accountant Anthea Rossignole and environmental biologist Shay Sumoto discover that it's never an easy commute on the Freeway of Love. But there are soft shoulders, merging traffic, and it's slippery when wet... (Lesbian Romance Novel)

Touchwood - 30th Anniversary Edition

A pre-Stonewall survivor. An out, proud woman of the Gay 90s. Decades separate them. Passion – and books – ignite them. Even when the world disapproves, love finds a way. *The author's cut of this beloved classic.* (Lesbian Romance Novel)

About the Author

Karin Kallmaker has been exclusively devoted to lesbian fiction since the publication of her first novel in 1989. As an author first published by the storied Naiad Press, she has been fortunate to be mentored by a number of editors, including Katherine V. Forrest.

In addition to multiple Lambda Literary Awards, she has been featured as a Stonewall Library and Archives Distinguished Author. Other accolades include the Ann Bannon Popular Choice and other awards for her writing, as well as the selection as a Trailblazer by the Golden Crown Literary Society. She is best known for novels such as *Painted Moon*, *Substitute for Love*, *Simply the Best*, *Maybe Next Time*, and *The Kiss that Counted*.

The California native is the mother of two and blogs at *Romance and Chocolate*. She adores ice cream, coffee, Tim Tams, and more ice cream. Connect with her on social media: search for "Kallmaker" — there's only one, which is definitely for the best.

Printed in Great Britain
by Amazon

29712443R00126